Breaking Free

BESTSELLING AUTHOR
ISABEL LUCERO

SOUTH RIVER UNIVERSITY #3
BY
ISABEL LUCERO

One

TREVOR

"IT'S JUST ONE NIGHT," Jayden tells me. "And it's only two hours away."

"Yeah, but on our rival's campus? The fucking Hornets?" I make a face as I shove my foot into my tennis shoe.

"Yeah, I know, but I got a friend who told me about this party. It's gonna be huge," he says, spraying some cologne on before checking himself out in the mirror.

"I'm obviously gonna go, but I'm talking shit to every football player I see. You know we play them first this season, right?"

"Yeah, and we're gonna whoop their ass."

Jayden's one of the best wide receivers we have on our team at South River, and I'm the best running back. With our friend Dex as QB, and a well-rounded team, we're set to win the national championship this year, no problem.

"Marco's not gonna be quarterback this season," Jayden says. "Hurt his shoulder."

"Damn. Who is it now? Luke?"

"Yep, but he's pretty good."

"And of course they have Jimmy Watts at receiver now. He's fast."

"We're still the better team," he says with confidence.

"All right," I say, shoving my wallet in my pocket. "I'm ready. Let's go get drunk."

"My man," Jayden says with a grin, giving me a fist bump before we leave my place.

We take Jayden's white Jeep Grand Cherokee and blast music the whole way there. When we pull up to the frat house where the party's being held, music blasts from inside, pouring out of every open window and door this place has. Cars line both sides of the street, and people are outside on the balcony of the second level, plastic cups in hand and smiles on their faces.

"Who do you know here?" I ask Jayden.

"A few people, actually, but this chick I'm talking to invited me out. Do you know Kristina Mathis?"

I scrunch my face. "I think so."

"Anyway, she goes to our school, but her best friend goes here."

"I see."

Jay checks his phone. "All right. She's inside. Let's go."

We head up the driveway and a few people smile and say *hey*, mostly to Jayden, who seems to know everybody no matter where we go.

"You've been here before, I take it."

He smiles. "A few times. Dex used to come with me before he got tied down."

"Oh, so I'm your second choice?" I joke.

"You're my favorite second choice, though."

"Whatever," I say with a laugh.

Inside, the music thumps so loud I can barely hear Jayden when he speaks. It's only because he gestures toward the kitchen that I know he probably said something about getting a drink.

It doesn't take long before we spot a couple of the football guys and end up getting caught up in conversation about the upcoming season while we down our beers and take a couple shots. Amongst the shit talking, we also discuss the other teams before Jimmy says something that catches my attention.

"He's leaving us for y'all."

"Wait, what?" I ask. "Who are we talking about?"

"This kid, uhh...Hernandez. He was second string last year, didn't see much play time until the end of the season. He's good, though, and getting better."

"What's his position?"

"Running back." Jimmy grins. "Gonna be gunning for your spot, Campbell."

I roll my eyes. "Yeah, right."

"Why the transfer?" Jayden asks.

The guys shrug and the topic is dropped, so we go about our drinking. Within an hour and a half, Jayden finds a girl he knows and disappears for a while. I end up playing drinking games with Jimmy and Marco for a while, and it isn't until my vision begins to blur that I realize my bladder's about to burst.

"Gotta take a piss," I tell them, leaving the table.

It takes a few minutes to find the bathroom, but when I do, it's because there's a line of four people in the hall.

"Is this the only bathroom?" I ask, my words strung together.

A redheaded girl gives me a once over before answering. "Someone's puking in the other one."

I grimace. "And in this one?"

"Having sex, I think," she says with a shrug, like it's normal.

I hurry back to Marco since I know he lives here. "Dude,

tell me I can use a bathroom on the second floor. You got people fucking and puking in the ones down here."

"Aw, come on," he complains, standing up. "Head upstairs, turn right. Second door on the left."

As he rushes off to handle the bathroom problems, I jog upstairs, trying to remember his directions.

The house is pretty big, but I'm sure it won't be too hard to find a bathroom. I'm about to open a door when I hear a girl moan Jayden's name. Well, at least I know where he is.

I try the next door, but it's locked. "Give me a minute," a guy yells.

"I don't have a minute," I bite back, almost ready to pull my dick out and piss in a deserted plastic cup.

I open all the doors, searching for another bathroom, and get lucky with one tucked away in the corner. As soon as I free myself from my jeans, I hardly get time to aim before my bladder lets loose. Midstream I realize how hot and muggy it is in here, and then the shower curtain is yanked back, and a naked, muscular, wet man stands there staring at me like I'm crazy.

"What the fuck are you doing?" he growls.

"Uh, taking a piss," I answer, averting my eyes and making sure I don't pee all over the floor.

Out of my peripheral vision, I see him step out and then hear him snatch a towel off the rack behind me. "There's three other bathrooms in here."

"All of them were occupied. Give me a minute and I'll be outta your hair."

He steps up to the sink, standing at my side. My eyes flicker to him briefly, gazing just long enough to notice he's wrapped a towel around his waist.

"Why aren't you downstairs partying?" I ask, tucking myself back in my pants.

"I'm not in the mood." His voice lacks any emotion.

I flush the toilet and turn to face him. Water still clings to his bronze skin, and his dark hair is slicked back with one little tendril falling over his forehead.

He's thick with muscles and tall—bigger than me by a few inches and several pounds, and he's extremely attractive. His jaw is angular and his cheekbones sharp. When I meet his gaze in the mirror, I realize I've been staring at him for way too long. I blame the alcohol. I told myself months ago not to get drunk and make dumb decisions. I've been there and done that. More than once.

The last time I got really drunk, I ended up having a brief hookup with my friend Renzo, and then I was embarrassed and ashamed, feeling like I used him to experiment, and it led to several days of awkwardness before we determined we were better off as friends.

However, it solidified what I was curious about—I definitely like guys. But besides Renzo and his boyfriend, Ronan, nobody knows.

It's not like I think my closest friends will judge me. Ronan and Renzo are gay, Jayden's bi, and nobody in our circle cares. However, I'm unsure of my other friends, and the guys on the team. Sure, Jay's on the football team, too, but his personality is more of the I-don't-give a-shit-what-you-think-of-me type, while I'm exactly the opposite. Plus there's my family, and I have zero idea how they might react to their only son being gay.

"Are you just gonna stand there and stare at me?"

His deep voice pulls me out of my thoughts. I lick my lips. "Can I wash my hands?"

He takes a step back, but doesn't leave much room between us. As I hold my hands under the water, I can almost feel him touching my back. My eyes travel up to the mirror as I massage in the soap, and I find him checking me out.

I clear my throat as I rinse off the suds and meet his stare.

Warm brown eyes meet my green ones and then he licks his bottom lip.

"You're not from here."

"No. I'm from South River."

Something flashes in his eyes and his lips pull into a tiny smirk. "Hmm."

When I turn around to look for a towel to dry my hands on, I realize the only one in here is wrapped around his waist.

"Well, I guess I'll let you get back to it," I say stupidly, wiping my wet hands on my jeans.

He doesn't move from in front of the door, so I take a step forward and reach for the knob, my head angling in his direction.

"How drunk are you?" he questions, catching me off guard.

"Uhh...a little."

His eyes move to my mouth and I wet my lips with a swipe of my tongue.

"Who are you here with?"

"My friend."

Why am I standing here, so close to him, answering questions? I should just shove him out of the way and leave. Who even is this guy? Why the sudden inquiry?

"Boyfriend?" he questions.

My brows dip in the middle. "No."

He shifts, turning to face me, his shoulder resting against the door. "Why don't you come to my room with me?"

I swallow thickly, my eyes trained on his mouth as he talks. Confusion and desire war with themselves as I think over what he just said. Alcohol has already impaired me, so I'm definitely not in the right mind to make sound decisions, but who says all decisions need to be good ones?

"Why?" I ask, frozen in place, my hand on the doorknob.

"To help me forget," he says huskily, coming even closer.

"Forget what?" I whisper, already leaning in.

"My fucked up life."

"How do..." I begin to ask *how do you know I'm gay,* but he shuts me up when he shoves me against the wall and pins his hips against mine.

"You've been checking me out since you walked in here, don't get shy now."

He cages me in when he braces his arms on either side of me, and my cock comes to life, straining against the zipper of my jeans. I know he feels it when he releases a sexy groan and pushes into me further.

My chest heaves as he slowly leans in, and when his lips brush against mine, any rational thought flees my brain, and I only care about what he tastes like and what his body will feel like under my hands.

This guy, whose name I don't even know, devours my mouth in the sexiest way. The kiss starts slowly, his lips pressing against mine in soft pecks, and then his tongue slides in, tangling with mine in a sensual dance. As soon as I moan, his right hand grabs the back of my head, his long fingers cradling my neck as his thumb aligns with my jaw. His grip is firm as he deepens the kiss, sucking on my tongue before his other hand travels under my shirt.

"Touch me," he growls, and it's then that I realize my arms are frozen at my sides.

I bring them up and splay my fingers across his abs and run my hands up to his chest before I let them travel around to his back, pulling him into me.

He steps back. "That's not really what I meant." His hand goes to his towel, and in a half a second, the white cotton material drops to the floor, leaving him completely naked.

"Oh."

I've had one experience with a guy, and that was my drunken hookup with Renzo. Well, we made out one time after, but it was thirty seconds at best. The alcohol-induced encounter was us making out and me sucking his dick. That's it. No touching, groping, licking, and not much talking if I'm being honest.

He smirks before undoing my pants, shoving them down my thighs. His large hand gropes my erection through my underwear before he pushes those down, too.

When he wraps his fingers around my cock, I close my eyes and drop my head against the wall. "Oh shit."

"Mm," he moans, coming closer and nuzzling my neck with his scratchy beard. "You're already dripping for me."

"Oh God," I moan.

"Be a good boy and suck my cock and maybe I'll let you come next."

His words send a jolt of desire up my spine. I should probably be offended that he called me a good boy, but something about his tone and the way he stroked my dick when he said it turned me on even more. Now all I want to do is please him so I can get my own release.

I bite my lip as I look into his dark eyes and then slowly drop to my knees. His cock is massive, long and thick, with a few veins straining against the tight skin. He runs his hand through my blond hair and I open my mouth and take him between my lips.

Having only done this once, I'm terrified he's going to realize how inexperienced I am and put a stop to this. With one hand on his muscled thigh, I use my other one to stroke his length, taking him as deep into my mouth as I can.

He begins fucking my face, gripping my hair tightly in his fist, and the grunts and groans let me know he's enjoying himself.

My cock throbs and leaks as I hollow my cheeks and suck on his crown before I let my tongue travel the underside of his shaft.

"Fuck." He grips his erection. "Open your mouth and stick out your tongue."

I don't hesitate to obey, something deep inside me loving that I don't have to wonder what to do next. He slaps his cock against my tongue and then strokes himself while staring into my eyes.

"I'm gonna come in your mouth."

It's not a question, so I don't say anything. I just keep my mouth open and my tongue out, and several seconds later jets of hot cum land on my tongue and chin.

With one hand on the wall behind me, he leans over, giving me every drop of his release. When he's done, he reaches down and grabs a hold of my neck, pulling me up.

His thumb swipes some of his cum from my chin and he pushes it into my mouth. "Good boy."

My heart hammers in my chest and my entire body feels like it's about to burst into flames. When his hand wraps around my cock and strokes, I think I might shatter, but when he leans into me and licks more of his cum off my chin before sticking his tongue into my mouth, I do. I explode and come all over his hand and thigh without any warning.

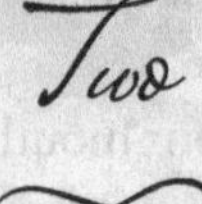

TREVOR

JAYDEN and I ended up staying the night at the apartment of the girl he hooked up with. After my somewhat embarrassing moment in the bathroom, where I came all over the hand of a man whose name I don't know after he only stroked me a handful of times, I didn't see him again.

I awkwardly and swiftly cleaned myself up and fastened my jeans as he casually stood there, naked and confident, and almost smug.

I muttered a goodbye before rushing down the hall and back downstairs, searching for Jay so we could leave.

Now it's ten past ten and I'm dressed and ready to go after having an uncomfortable night of sleep on a couch that was way too small for my frame.

"It was nice seeing you," Jayden drawls, his muscular arm draped around Erin's shoulders.

"You too. I might be down there in a month or so. Let's meet up," she replies with a grin, stretching up on her tiptoes to kiss him.

"You know how to get in touch." He spanks her ass, making her squeal before finding my gaze. "You ready?"

"Yep."

"Bye, Trent," Erin says with a wave, making Jayden snort.

"Bye, Erin."

"Oh. It's Evelyn."

"Ah."

Jayden grabs my shoulder and spins me around, laughing as we make our way outside. "Guess I didn't properly introduce you two."

"You probably don't need to."

He chuckles deeply. "You're probably right."

"How far away is the frat house?"

"We only have to walk a block," he answers, pulling his phone out of his pocket to read a text. "So what did you get up to last night?"

Memories flash in my mind. Naked man stepping out of the shower. Said man checking me out as I washed my hands. Towel-clad man asking me to spend some time in his room, and then all but forcing me to my knees to suck him off before making me come in a matter of seconds.

Heat travels up my neck, reaching my face as I think about it. I turn away so Jayden won't notice.

"Not much. Got drunk."

He's quiet for several seconds before he jumps in front of me, walking backwards as he studies my face. "You're lying." His laugh is loud and full of joy. "You hooked up. Who was it with?"

I meet his stare. "I didn't hook up with anyone."

His megawatt smile widens, showing off his pearly white teeth. "You know I know everything, right? And if I don't know it now, I will find out."

I roll my eyes. "There's nothing to find out."

"Bro, it's not like I'm gonna judge you for hooking up with someone you don't know. We're in fucking college. It's like a right of passage or something."

I chuckle and shake my head. "Believe me, I've already experienced that right of passage. Remember those chicks from the party at my house several months ago?"

His brows furrow. "Which ones?"

"Exactly. I don't know. The following morning Dex told me I was making out with three girls. I don't know who they were. I was shit-faced."

Jayden laughs, unlocking his car with the key FOB, and the subject is dropped. After he starts the car, he sends a text to someone and then drops his phone in the cup holder.

"Men."

I turn to look at him. "What?"

"Just this guy," he says, pulling away from the road. "We messed around a few times a while back and he's wanting to meet up, but I'm not into it. I've told him a few times, but he's not taking the hint."

"You don't like him anymore?"

"I like him well enough, I guess, but he's in the closet. It's not really what I go for."

My pulse spikes. "Why's that?"

He glances at me before turning his attention to the road. "Look, don't get me wrong, I get being in the closet. I was until two years ago, but now that I'm free to be me, I don't want to hide again. Kind of like how Renzo felt. You remember what he went through before."

"Right." I stare out the window, thinking about how I may never have a chance with anyone if I'm still in the closet. "So this guy just wants to hook up in secret?"

"Yeah, which is fine if it's just a hookup. I can do that one time and not think about it again, but we had several hookups, and I started to like him, which in itself is crazy, so I cut it off."

"You don't think he'll come out?"

"Mm." He rubs his chin. "His family is from the middle

east. All he's told me is that they'd never allow him to marry or love a man openly. I don't think he'll come out, and that makes me sad for him, but it's also why I won't tie myself to him either."

"I get it." I'm silent for a little while, but then I ask, "Were you afraid to come out?"

He laughs. "Are you kidding? I was terrified! Did you not sense my fear when I told you guys?"

I grin. "No, actually. You seemed so confident."

"Fake it till you make it, I guess," he says with another laugh. "I was definitely nervous, but I knew I was attracted to both guys and girls when I was like eleven, and I kept it a secret until I was eighteen. I couldn't hide it any longer. My parents took it pretty decently, I guess. They were both shocked and questioned me several times on whether I was sure or not. But I was eighteen when I came out, and on my way to college, so what were they gonna do? Ground me?" He laughs. "Once they knew, I had a little more confidence telling my friends."

I chew on my lip, wanting to ask more questions but knowing it would likely out me, because why would I care so much about how it feels to come out?

"Well, are you looking to settle down anytime soon, anyway? You seem pretty happy just doing your thing."

"Ah," he chuckles, his smile bright. "Eventually. I am pretty content not having to worry about committing."

The conversation eventually shifts to football, as it usually does with us. "So, we're getting a new guy," I say.

He laughs. "Don't let Watts get to you, man. I doubt this guy is gonna take your spot."

"I'm not worried," I tell him, though I'm not a hundred percent sure about that. "I mean, I know we have to have four on roster, but me and Deshawn have been the starters, and Travis and Dan are pretty good for backups."

"Well, Dan's gone," Jayden says.

"Right, but what if this new guy is even better than me or Deshawn and he gets put out on the field as a starter?"

Jay laughs. "Sounds like you are a little worried."

"I'm just not trying to get benched for some new kid who doesn't even know this team."

"You'll be fine," he says with all the confidence in the world. "So, tell me who you hooked up with. Was she a brunette? You like brunettes, don't you?"

I spend the rest of our time in the car avoiding telling him about my bathroom hookup. I don't even know why I don't tell him. He's not gonna judge me for liking guys, but every time I open my mouth with the thought to just say, *I'm gay*, I freeze up and panic and can't bring myself to spit the words out.

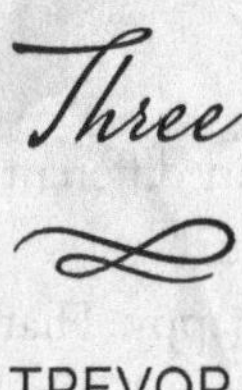

Three

TREVOR

"ANOTHER FUCKING YEAR," Renzo gripes as we meet up on the central campus right outside one of the towering buildings.

"Yep. Just one more to go. Where's Ronan?"

"He's on the north campus right now."

Dex and Violet stroll by so I lift my chin and raise my hand, and Violet waves excitedly, running to give Zo a hug.

"This campus is huge!"

"You know where all your classes are?" Zo asks.

"I'll figure it out. Even if I'm late to all of them."

"You hear about the new guy who got on the team without having to attend tryouts?" Dex asks me as Zo and Vi talk.

"Yeah, me and Jay heard about him at a party last weekend. You know anything about him?"

Dex shakes his head. "Not much. I just know he's a running back."

"So I hear," I groan.

Dex laughs and slaps my shoulder. "Don't worry, man. You're still my favorite RB."

"Yeah, yeah."

"Gotta go," Vi says, glancing at her watch.

"Me too," Dex says, leaning down to give her a kiss. "I'll text you later."

"Okay. Love you."

"Love you."

They split up to go in different directions and I look at Zo. "Is it still weird for you?"

He shrugs. "They're happy. That's all I care about."

We head to the building that holds our first classes of the day, and I think back to when Renzo found out about Vi and Dex. It was quite the scene at a party when he found them locked in a bathroom together. Though it was ugly for a little while, Zo and Dex were able to patch things up. Which is good, considering they've been best friends since they were in elementary school.

Inside, we split up to go to our individual classes, and I don't see any of my friends until lunch.

"Did anyone have Professor Gibbs. God, what a dick," Ronan complains before taking a bite of his club sandwich.

"Nah, but I have Professor Hansley for social science and he has the most monotone voice. I swear I'm gonna fall asleep in that class a few times," I reply.

Jayden pops a chip in his mouth and chews. "I got a glimpse at this hot as fuck professor today. I don't have him, but fuck if I want to."

Renzo snorts. "Is it Knight?"

"How did you know?" Jayden exclaims.

Ronan grins and eyes Renzo. "Yes, how did you know?"

"Oh please," Zo scoffs. "If you saw him you'd know. He's definitely attractive."

"Mmhmm," Ronan murmurs, a small grin on his lips.

"You're still my number one," Zo tells him, draping an arm over his shoulders and planting a kiss on his temple.

"Where's Vi and Dex?" Jay asks.

"Probably off scr—" I cut myself off when I see Renzo narrow his eyes at me. "Studying. Probably studying."

Jay and Ronan laugh.

"Anyway, gotta run," I say, gathering my trash. "See ya in practice," I tell Jayden.

"Yessir."

~

My next two classes seem to drag, but that's probably because I'm too focused on getting to practice to see what this new guy is about. We had practice in the summer, but since he's new, we haven't seen him. I'm internally hoping he's some half-ass running back who doesn't have a lot of speed or can't hold onto the ball, and therefore I won't have anything to worry about.

In the locker room, voices bounce off the walls as a group of guys laugh boisterously at something someone said, and as another group talks loudly about some party they went to. I'm stripping out of my clothes and getting ready to don my practice gear when the doors slam closed and heavy footsteps approach.

I yank up my black football pants and turn my head to the right when I see someone round the corner. I have to do a double take when my eyes meet a familiar face.

What the fuck?

"What's wrong?" Jayden asks from behind me. Apparently I didn't just think those three words.

I don't answer him, because my gaze is focused on the naked man from the bathroom at Grand Valley. He doesn't look nearly as surprised to see me. Instead, he does a slow perusal of my naked torso and then grins.

Shit.

Shit, shit, shit.

He strolls right up next to me and leans his hulking shoulder on the locker while studying me in a way that makes me break out in a sweat. "Well, hello, stranger."

I clear my throat, my eyes shifting to Jayden who's watching us with confusion marring his face.

"Hey." I go for nonchalance, reaching for my shirt. "I'm guessing you're the transplant."

He snorts. "I guess you could say that."

Jayden stands up and gets between us. "I'm Jayden, or Jay. One of the receivers. And you are?"

The Greek god smiles. "Dominic. Or Dom. New running back."

"Hernandez?" I blurt, remembering the guys from the party talking about him.

His dark eyes find mine, his mouth pulling up into an amused grin. "Heard about me?"

I scoff. "Hardly."

"This is Trevor. Another running back."

"Interesting," Dominic says. "Trevor." He says my name like he wants to know how it feels on his tongue, all the while, unabashedly checking me out.

I pull my pads on. "Better hurry up and change. We're out on the field in five."

"I was just with Coach. I'm sure he'll give me a few extra minutes."

I don't respond, I just quickly get my cleats on and grab my jersey, walking away because I don't want to be around when he starts undressing.

"Do you know him?" Jayden asks, running after me.

"No."

"Uh." He chuckles. "Seems like he knows you, or at least wants to. Did you notice him checking you out? You're gonna have to break his little heart."

"I think I saw him at the party, but I don't remember much." I yank my jersey over my head. "I don't think he was checking me out. Not like that. I'm just competition. Seems full of himself, though, huh?"

Jayden looks back. "Shit, he has every right to be. He's sexy as fuck."

I scoff and as soon as we hit the doors to head to the field, I realize I forgot my gloves.

"Shit. I gotta get my gloves. Meet you out there."

I jog back to the locker and spot Dominic changing nearby. Great, we're locker neighbors.

He watches me approach, but I do my best to pretend I don't notice his chiseled body as I pull open my locker.

"I think I like you better drunk," he says.

I blow out a breath, closing the locker after I get my gloves. "Look, Dominic."

"Dom," he says.

"I was drunk and what happened between us was just a product of me making inebriated decisions that I normally wouldn't make if I was in my right mind."

He stands at full height. "A drunken mistake?"

"Right," I say with a nod, finding it hard to make eye contact with him.

"You said you were a *little* drunk, and you weren't too inebriated to get your dick up."

I swivel my head around, making sure nobody's in here. "Okay, but I'm not...out. Nobody knows. Well, two people know, but really, nobody knows."

He chews on his lip, studying me. "I see."

"Yeah, so don't say anything to anyone. Please. We can't start anything. I didn't expect to ever see you again, let alone here, trying to take my spot."

Dominic finishes dressing and closes his locker. He stops at my side and looks at me. "Who said I wanted to start anything with someone who came on my hand in five seconds?" He clucks his tongue. "I like my men to last a little longer than that."

He strolls away, leaving me fuming.

Four

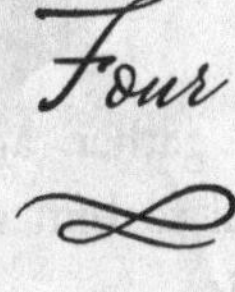

TREVOR

HE'S GOOD. Dammit.

Dominic runs fast, holds on to the ball like he's got glue on his fingers, and knows how to juke the other players in order to get around them.

I can't say I'm too surprised, because obviously Coach knew about his skills in order to let him on the team. I wonder if he went to the other campus and watched him. Anyway, I can't help but be disappointed, because there was a small part of me that hoped he was mediocre at best. I can't help but question why he wasn't a starter on his last team.

On top of his talent as a player, he seems to be well-liked by the guys already, which only annoys me for some reason.

I watch him jog to the sidelines to get some water, and stare as he squirts it into his mouth. After he gulps it down, he pours some on his inky black hair, the water cascading over his forehead. He shakes his head before pushing his hand through his hair, moving it out of his face, then he locks eyes with me and smirks.

Even though he can't hear me, I scoff and turn my head,

focusing my attention on the field as Coach talks to a group of players.

"Hey."

My head snaps to the side as Dominic approaches, leering at me.

"What?"

"All right, everyone gather around," Coach Beckett announces, drawing us all to him and getting me out of a conversation with Dominic.

I jog over and find a spot next to Jay and Dex, and listen to Coach's speech about his expectations and what we need to work on.

Dominic stands across from me, watching me in a way that makes me uncomfortable. Uncomfortable because if anyone else is paying attention, I think it's obvious he's checking me out. I don't want to have to answer any questions about the new guy being attracted to me.

I don't even know why he's looking at me like this, considering the shit he said in the locker room. First of all, how dare he? I was drunk, horny, and turned on beyond all belief, especially after having him fuck my mouth and lick his cum into my mouth. It's not like I'm a minute man. It was just the situation. I haven't been with many guys. Two, including him, to be exact. And I'm starting to learn just how much I like it, so excuse the fuck out of me for coming somewhat quick.

My face burns as I think about it, getting angrier at him for even trying to make me feel bad. If he doesn't want to be with me, then he shouldn't stare at me the way he is.

"Whoa, what's goin' on?"

Dex's voice pulls me out of my head and I realize I was glaring at Dominic.

"What?" I ask.

"You were looking at him like you wanted to kill him," Dex says.

"Oh man, you should've seen how he was looking at Trev in the locker room, though," Jay says with a laugh. "I think he's sweet on Campbell here."

"Oh?" Dex asks, eyebrows raised.

I shake my head and realize the group has been dismissed, so we start walking to the locker room. "I don't think he was checking me out."

"He seems like a good guy," Dex says with a shrug. "Pretty good on the field, too."

I try to keep my eyeroll to myself. I don't want to look jealous. "He's okay."

Jay and Dex share a look and then laugh.

"I'm not jealous," I say. "I just...I don't know. He seems cocky."

"Well, regardless of all that," Jayden says. "When he comes on to you and you have to turn him down, send him my way, yeah? Because I can have a good time with him."

"We don't even know if he's gay," Dex says.

I do, but it's not like I'm gonna say that.

"Y'all can keep talking about him all you want. I'm hittin' the showers," I say, jogging into the building.

～

I'm not able to get right into the shower like I want, because Coach has another little speech while we undress, and then he calls me into his office.

"Yeah, Coach?" I ask.

"I wanted to have a quick word with you." He sits down behind his desk and moves some papers around, leaving me in suspense.

"Did I do something?"

"No, no. Nothing like that. As you know, Hernandez is new on the team."

"Oh. Yeah."

"I know y'all play the same position, but that doesn't mean there has to be any animosity. He's in a unique situation and it wasn't his choice to come here. Well, it was, but it wasn't." He waves his hand. "Anyway, that's beside the point. He doesn't need to be shown around town or anything, but if he needs help around campus or something, give him a hand."

"Coach, he's grown. I'm sure he can figure it out himself."

He pins me with a look. "Trevor, I asked you, because I know you're a good guy. Look, the team is like a family, and he's new. Just make him feel welcome. Sometimes people need support more than you know."

I sigh, crossing my arms. Coach has never asked this of me before, so I'm assuming there's a reason. Maybe he knows him. A friend of the family or something. Whatever the reason, it's fucking weird, but what am I gonna say? No? He's my coach and has the power to bench me if he wants. It's not like he'll know if I'm not helping him.

"Sure, Coach."

"Thanks, now get out of here."

I chuckle as I leave his office and head back to my locker. Most of the team is gone, some are already showered and getting dressed.

"Hey, man. Nicola's Pizza. Meet us there," Jay yells as he pops around the corner, heading out the door.

"All right."

I grab my flip flops, shower bag, and a towel before heading to the showers, passing Jacob on the way in.

"You goin' to Nicola's?" he asks.

"Yeah, I'm gonna shower real quick and head over."

"Cool. See ya there."

Inside, the showers are split up into doorway size cutouts, lining the walls with curtains to close us in. I find one and turn the water on, letting it warm up before I step in. While I wait, I strip out of my clothes and hang my towel on the hook outside.

Once I'm clean I pull open the curtain, reaching for my towel, only to find Dominic traveling down the corridor, fully dressed.

"Looks like the tables have turned," he says with a grin.

I quickly wrap the towel around my waist and turn my back on him. "Whatever, man."

"It's not like I haven't seen it before."

My head swivels from side-to-side, wondering if anyone else is in here. I think I hear a shower running on the other side of the room.

"First of all, keep your voice down. Second of all, you won't see it again."

He chuckles, walking alongside me as I try to leave him behind. "Sure."

"I thought you didn't want to start something with someone like me."

"Sounds like you're a little upset about that," he says, his voice laced with amusement.

"I'm not."

"I've been thinking about it," he states, leaning against the lockers as I put my stuff away and grab my clothes.

"Oh yeah? On the field?"

"I can do multiple things at once. So, I was thinking, we already started something. Might as well continue. I'm a generous man and I'm willing to give you another chance."

My eyes snap to his face as he grins at me and my anger burns hot. "You know what? You're a cocky son of a bitch. Regardless of what you want to do, I don't want to. So thanks for your chance," I snarl, "But I don't want it."

He pushes away from the lockers, walking toward me until my back slams into the same set of lockers, the sound loud and echoey.

"I think you do want it."

His body pushes into mine and he angles his head, looking down at me while I try to control my breathing.

"You're wrong. You were simply a drunken encounter. A one-night stand."

He slides his tongue slowly across his bottom lip, his eyes boring into mine. "I don't think so."

I turn my head to the side, afraid whoever was in the shower will walk out any minute now. "Can you back the fuck up?"

"Why? You clearly like me being this close to you," he murmurs, dragging the tip of his nose down the bridge of mine. "I can feel it."

I shove him back and turn around to pull a shirt out of the locker and bring it over my head. "I'm gonna need you to stop staring at me the way you do, especially around people. Jayden's already caught on."

"Why do I have to stop? I'm not in the closet."

"Yeah, but I don't need any questions to come up."

I pull my boxer-briefs on while still wearing my towel, and then drop it to put my jeans on.

"Then maybe *you* need to focus on not staring at *me*."

"I'm looking at you with contempt. It's different."

He laughs. "Sure."

I sit on the bench behind me to put on my socks and shoes while he towers over me. "Look, I'm not sure when I'm gonna come out. I have zero plans on how to do it, so I don't need you here trapping me against lockers and looking at me like you've seen me naked."

"But I have." He grins.

I huff. "It won't happen again. I only let it happen because you weren't from here, but here you are. A fucking thorn in my side already."

"I could be a prick in your ass if you want. Maybe your mouth."

"Do you not listen?" I exclaim, standing up.

His large hand lands on my shoulder and shoves me back down as he stands in front of me. I look up at him, shell-shocked, and then he runs his fingers through my hair. "But you look so good like this," he says, his voice low and husky. "Looking up at me with those green eyes and parted lips, like you're just waiting for me to tell you what to do. Admit it, you enjoyed yourself with me."

I open my mouth to say something even though I have no idea what to tell him. He's not wrong, but there's no way I'm admitting that to him.

He doesn't give me time to argue, because the hand that was in my hair quickly curves around my cheek and his thumb pushes between my lips. On instinct, like I don't have a mind of my own, I close my mouth around it and suck gently.

Dominic smirks, victorious. "I knew it."

Annoyance and frustration—not only with him but with myself—blooms and explodes, and with all the strength I can muster, I push him back after jolting to my feet, making him stumble into the lockers.

But of course he isn't offended or mad. He just gives me a crooked smile.

"Hey, y'all coming to Nicola's?" Marcus asks, walking in from the shower room.

"Nicola's?" Dom questions.

"It's a pizza parlor. A group of us are heading over. You should come. Get to know everyone a little better."

I like Marcus, but all I want to do is punch him in the mouth for telling Dominic about our plans.

I slam my locker closed. "I'll see you there, Marcus."

I've only taken a handful of strides before I hear Dominic's voice say, "Yeah, me too."

Outside, I walk with purpose as I head to my car, but Dominic follows. "Hey, think you could give me a ride?"

"No."

He laughs. "Come on."

"Definitely no."

"How am I supposed to get there?"

"I'm sure you have a car, don't you?"

"Not today. I needed to leave it with someone."

"Sounds like a lie."

"It's not."

It takes several minutes to get to the parking lot and Dominic continues to walk with me in silence until I stop at my red Mazda CX-30. I unlock it and throw my stuff in the backseat, doing my best to ignore his very large presence.

I open the driver's side door and see his ridiculous faux pout and pleading hands on the other side.

"Get in and don't talk to me."

Five

TREVOR

ONCE I PARK in front of Nicola's, I quickly get out and dart for the door, leaving Dominic behind me. I'd like to say the ride was quiet, but he talked almost the entire time. He didn't say anything important, just enough to annoy me.

I spot our group in the far corner in the oversized booth, everyone already eating. "Hey," I greet, pushing into the booth next to Jayden. "I'm starving."

"Y'all come together?" he asks quietly, eyes focused on Dominic who's approaching the table.

I sigh, snatching a piece of meat-lovers from the wooden pizza plate. "Don't ask," I say with a growl.

Jayden chuckles. "Hey, man," he says, greeting the insufferable Dominic. "Glad you could make it."

"I'm not gonna turn down pizza," he says, his eyes scanning the area for a place to sit.

Leo, one of our tight ends, grabs the plastic cup and slurps down the rest of his drink through the straw before saying, "I'm leaving. You can have my spot. Gotta meet up with my girl."

Me and Jayden have to stand up to let him out, and when

we take our seats, I realize we have to slide over to the right, giving Dominic the spot to my left.

He plops down next to me, his thigh pushing against mine.

"So, what's up with you?" Jayden asks.

"What do you mean?" he asks.

"What's your story?" When Dominic stays quiet, Jayden puts his pizza down and grins. "So, for me, my story is that I moved here three years ago. I'm from Illinois, but South River offered me more when it came to athletics. Not only do I play football, but I'm on the wrestling team. I'm in a frat—K. A. P. You know, shit like that."

Dominic chuckles. "Ah. Well, I don't play any other sports, and I'm from here. Went to school up at Grand Valley before transferring."

"Boo! Fucking Hornets," Tim, our kicker, teases.

"Rival teams. How do you feel playing for the Wildcats now?" Jay asks.

He shrugs. "Feel like I'm gonna win."

The table erupts into cheers, annoying everyone in the restaurant for the next thirty seconds.

"I like you already, man," Shea says, holding his cup up to him.

I scoff under my breath and focus on my food, but of course Dominic hears me and knocks his knee into mine.

"What's your story, Trevor?" Dominic asks, enunciating my name.

I angle my head over my shoulder and glare at him before I remember people are watching. "Not much. From here, go to school here, play football."

Jayden hits me in the arm. "Come on, man. That's not it. He also throws the best parties. Well, besides the one my frat throws. Though you may find him drunk and making out with multiple chicks, but what's new in college?"

My eyes slide over to Dominic's face and I can't help but notice how his brows are reaching for his hairline as he stares at me. "Oh yeah? Making out with multiple girls at parties, huh? You don't seem the type."

Some of the guys laugh, but I grind my teeth, biting back my response.

"Don't worry, even if Campbell takes three girls for himself, the women always seem to outnumber us," Shea says.

Dominic raises his head and meets Shea's gaze. "Well, I'm gay, so that doesn't help me out at all."

The guys go quiet, maybe wondering if he's joking or not, but when he just takes a slice of pizza and bites a chunk out of it, Jayden chuckles.

"These guys are cool, don't worry," Jay says. "I'm bi and there's never been any major problems with most of the team."

"Major and most," Dominic says with a snort. "Sounds about right."

"There's always assholes," Jay says.

The guys liven up. "Sorry, I just didn't expect you to be gay," Tim says.

"Right, because of stereotypes." When they all go quiet again, Dominic laughs. "I'm fucking with you. Don't worry about it. It's not the first time I've shocked people. If you don't have a problem with my personal life, I don't have a problem with you. Plain and simple."

Conversation moves on after that, but I can't help but think about how confidently he came out and announced that to everyone. A football team that he's a new member of. He had no qualms, hesitation, or concerns. Is it really that easy?

An hour later, everyone starts leaving.

"All right, man. See you later," Jayden says, knocking his

fist against mine. "Dom, nice getting to know ya, bro. See you tomorrow."

I don't talk to Dominic until we're outside. "So I guess I'm taking you home."

"Don't sound so thrilled. It's all right. I'll catch the bus from here."

And now I feel bad. Great.

"It's fine. Really. I can take you."

His lips curl up on one side. "Don't change your tone now. It's okay. I'd rather take the bus."

"Do you live on campus? My place is nearby. It wouldn't be a hassle."

He begins walking away, but turns around and continues moving backward. "Careful. It's starting to sound like you want me to join you."

I roll my eyes. "Do you want a ride or not?"

His teeth drag across his bottom lip. "Do you?"

"You know what? Okay, fine. See you tomorrow."

His laugh hits my ears right before I open my car door. As much as he annoys the fuck out of me, I don't want to leave him stranded. I look back at him before I get in.

"Go, Campbell," he says with a chuckle. "I'm a big boy. I'll find my way."

With that, he turns on his heel and disappears around the building, and I hate that I wish he was still here, even if it just means we'd bicker the whole time.

DOMINIC

IT'S BEEN two weeks since I transferred and started school at South River, and it's a lot better than I thought it would be. The campus is a little bigger than my last one, and the athletic compound is definitely better. They clearly have more funding here.

That's not to say I didn't like Grand Valley. I enjoyed my time there and had good friends and a steady job. Football wasn't my top priority there, and I was content on the bench for the majority of the season, because my attention was on passing my classes and working my ass off.

Half my money was sent to my mom to make sure she had whatever she needed since my dad was a controlling, alcoholic asshole who didn't allow my mom to live freely.

I actually grew up an hour and a half away from South River, and as soon as I graduated high school I was quick to flee to Grand Valley just to get away from my dad, because I was afraid one of our fights would explode into something I couldn't come back from.

I begged my mom to leave him but she wouldn't. In one of his brief *I'll be better* moments, they decided to move to

South River for a new start, but I was already up at Grand Valley. I came here twice to visit, but only when I knew my dad wouldn't be around.

My dad died four weeks ago, and now I'm here for an indeterminate amount of time, but definitely until I graduate.

Mom needs my help. She hasn't had a job in years because my dad stopped allowing that when he was afraid her co-workers were getting in her head and giving her confidence to leave him. My dad was the sole breadwinner, and while she has some insurance coming her way, she's not going to get a lot.

For reasons I don't understand, she's actually grieving the prick. I don't know when she'll be ready to start looking for a job, so I'm here to help her financially and emotionally.

Because the coach at South River knew my parents, he was vaguely aware of the toxic situation I left behind, and when he found out my dad dropped dead of a heart attack, leaving my mom a widow so unexpectedly, he, along with my coach at Grand Valley, helped me get transferred here quickly while also getting me on the football team.

Coach Bennett here at South River came down to watch me play, and after talking to my coach, he allowed me on the team without having to attend their tryouts. My circumstances definitely helped. Thanks, Dad.

I got a job at one of the bars, because it's one of the few places that gives me more hours in the evening, since I'll be at school during the day. Because I don't know shit about being a bartender, I'll be a barback, which is just stocking, lifting heavy crates of alcohol, and cleaning. But the owner told me if I had time, to watch the bartenders and learn the drinks, and maybe I can eventually be a bartender.

Personally, I don't care what I do as long as it gets me money. I'm not in a place to be picky.

I walk down the hall of the small three bedroom house my

parents bought a couple years ago. It's not a bad house, but it could use some work. My mom sits at the round dining room table with a cup of coffee, staring into the steaming liquid.

"Hey, Ma."

Her head comes up slowly, eyes red-rimmed. "Hey. Want some coffee?"

I sit down next to her. "I'm good. How are you?"

She forces a tight smile. "I'm...fine."

I lay my hand on hers. "You gonna be okay today?"

"Yes, of course," she replies, pulling her hand out from under mine to give me a few taps. "I think I'll try to clean up a bit."

I nod, pressing my lips into a line. "I can help when I get back."

"Don't worry about me."

I don't bother explaining I'm worried because she hasn't showered in a week, hardly eats, and seems to be surviving on cat naps.

"I'll always worry. Call me if you need me," I tell her, standing up. "Ms. Anne next door is also willing to help if you need anything," I say, kissing her forehead.

"Antonio never liked her. Said she couldn't mind her own business."

I sigh, biting back what I really want to say. "She's nice and she's willing to help."

"Go ahead, baby," she says, shooing me away. "Don't be late."

Outside, I exhale a breath and spot Anne on her porch. The houses around here are pretty close, so it doesn't take me long to make my way over to her.

"Is she okay?" she asks.

I shrug. "About the same."

Anne frowns and looks at our house. She's probably in her late fifties or early sixties, and currently has rollers in her mostly white hair. She was quick to pull me to the side when I first arrived and told me she overheard lots of arguments and called the cops a couple times. She's not sad my dad's dead either. Said she knew he was an evil man. He even came over here and threatened her after the cops had left one night.

"I'll go over with some food in a little bit," she says.

"Thank you."

My mom's sister flew into town last week, and while she was here, I let her use my car, but now that she's back home with her family in New Mexico, I have the car back, so I hop in and start driving.

Going to school has become the bright spot in my life, if not for any other reason than I get to see Trevor and get him riled up just by looking at him.

Having him show up at my frat house right as I was packing up to leave was the gift I didn't know I needed. The death of my father affected me less than worrying how my mom was going to deal with his absence. But that, paired with a quick move, the stress of transferring, and starting over had me in a pretty shitty mood.

Trevor with his bright green, curious, and wandering eyes gave me something else to focus on, even if it was just for that short amount of time, but hopefully I can convince him to give me more.

Seven

DOMINIC

BECAUSE I CAN TELL he's trying his hardest to act like he doesn't notice me standing just two locker spaces away, I go out of my way to talk to him.

"Hey, Campbell."

His shoulders rise and fall with a deep breath and it brings a smile to my lips. I spot Jayden to my left, looking up at us with amusement in his eyes before he wanders off.

"What?" he responds, not bothering to glance in my direction.

"I was thinking you look familiar. Like maybe I've seen you before I moved here."

His head snaps in my direction, eyes narrowed. "You're mistaken," he all but snarls through gritted teeth.

The few guys nearby don't take notice of his obvious hostility, too wrapped up in their own conversations.

"All right, guys," Jayden says, popping around the corner. "Let's get our asses on the field before Coach makes us run extra miles."

"You need to fucking stop," Trevor says as we trail the rest of the team.

"Stop what?"

"You tell me. What's your fucking plan? You keep saying and doing these things, completely unconcerned with anyone hearing or seeing us."

My teeth briefly sink into my bottom lip. "Well, I don't care if anyone sees or hears me."

"That's the fucking problem. You're being selfish and only thinking of yourself. I told you I'm not out." His voice drops. "I don't want people knowing I did anything with you."

I slap my hand over my chest. "Ouch, Campbell. Embarrassed?" He huffs. "All right. Fine. I'll leave you alone."

"Good," he says after a few seconds before rushing ahead of me.

The truth of the matter is, I don't know him that well. I shouldn't care if he doesn't want anything to do with me. But his willingness to do what I say feeds my need for control unlike anyone else I've been with.

I've been with twinks and jocks, and nobody has so easily succumbed to my demands like Trevor has. He happily went along with my plans that night in the bathroom, and had we been anywhere but in the locker room that first day of practice, I know he would've dropped to his knees if I told him to.

On top of that, he's fucking sexy. He's athletic and muscular, but still lean. He's clean-cut without being a baby face. And of course, for my own selfish reasons, I want to be able to have someone take my mind off my current problems. He's the drug I want to take in order to escape reality, even if it's only for a small amount of time. Even if it'll destroy me.

Trevor says he wants me to leave him alone, but I know that's his fear talking. He's afraid he likes me too much, and not just because I'm me. I'm a man, and he's still coming to terms with that. I think he's afraid if I'm around too much he'll succumb to every natural instinct he has. He'll stare too long, smile in a way he shouldn't, blush when I say something, and submit when he should resist.

I'll give him what he thinks he wants until he comes to me. It's bound to happen.

~

"Hey, nice fucking run," Jayden says, slapping my shoulder as I get to the sidelines after scoring a touchdown.

"Thanks, man." I squirt water into my mouth and then stand there, catching my breath.

"Yeah, you made Mills fall down," he says with a laugh. "I'll be sure to give him shit for that later."

I shake my head as I chuckle. "He owes me a drink. I told him I'd shake him, but he said there was no way I'd get past him."

Jayden throws his head back with a boisterous laugh. "Fucking Mills. I'm gonna make him buy me a drink, too. So, you're twenty-one?"

"Yep."

"Dope. Let's hit up the bar. Me, you, Mills—since he's buying, and maybe a few others. That cool?"

"Yeah, definitely. Tonight? Because I have to work tomorrow."

"Probably. Hold up." He walks a few steps away and shouts to a few guys. "Yo, Mills, Shea! Wanna hit up Toast tonight?"

"Fuck yeah."

"Hell yeah."

"I'm inviting myself."

Responses are immediate and Jayden strolls back with a grin. "It's on."

"Toast?"

He laughs. "It's called A Toast Away, but nobody ever says

the whole thing. I know it's a weird name, but it's the best bar in the local area."

"Sounds good to me."

"Where do you work?" he asks.

"I guess the second best bar. Three Sheets."

Jayden laughs. "Maybe third best."

I spot Trevor staring in our direction, and I try not to overthink the look on his face, but if I had to guess, it seems like jealousy.

I gesture toward him and say, "What about Campbell?"

Jayden looks over at him. "Ah, well, he's still twenty."

"Shame."

Jayden angles his body, giving his back to Trevor so he can look right at me. "You got a thing for Trev or what?"

My eyes move from the scowling face of Trevor Campbell and meet Jayden's dark gaze. "He's nice to look at."

He chuckles. "Yeah, all right. I wouldn't get too caught up in Trevor. I know some other guys who are actually into dick, though."

I laugh. "Maybe I'll meet someone tonight."

"Shit, hopefully I do, too."

We laugh and talk for a couple more minutes before we're dismissed to head back into the locker room. I keep my steps unhurried as the rest of the team seems to be in a rush to get changed and leave to enjoy the weekend. Besides the plans for tonight, I don't have anything fun planned. My nights usually consist of making food and hoping my mom will actually eat some of it, while also trying to keep her in the living room instead of crawling into her bed.

I get she has to grieve. I may not understand why she's grieving an abusive alcoholic, but I know I can't force her to not care about the death of a man she spent most of her life with. I just want to make sure she's caring for herself. I want her to know she has a full life ahead of her. My parents were young when they had me, so she's only forty. She could find a man who loves her and treats her the way she should've always been treated.

So, I'm not in a rush to change and get home, and maybe that's wrong of me. I should want to be home with her, but half the time I am there, I don't think she notices. So I take my time getting to my locker and grabbing my bag to take to the showers.

Most of the guys choose to go home to shower since it's already the end of the day, but there's a few that shower here because they have to go to work right after.

"Give me your number," Jayden says, shoving his phone in my hand. "Shea, hold up," he yells toward the other door. "Anyway, I'll text you later about where to go. Or we can meet up."

"Sounds good," I say, handing the phone back to him.

He hits my shoulder with his fist before he jogs toward Shea. When I turn around, Trevor's watching me.

I think to say something, but decide not to. I just lift my chin and head to the showers, deciding to take my time getting clean.

When I turn the corner, I'm shocked to find Trevor sitting on the bench in front of the lockers, his legs bouncing while he waits.

I walk behind him and open my locker, ignoring his presence until he says, "We need to talk."

Eight

DOMINIC

"I DON'T THINK WE DO," I reply, shoving my shower bag into the locker and removing my clothes.

"What are you trying to do?" he asks, his voice thick with frustration.

"I'm trying to get dressed, Campbell. Then I'll be heading home, where I'll start getting ready to go out tonight. Is that okay with you?"

He jolts up, slamming my locker closed. "Enough with the smartass bullshit. Are you trying to piss me off? Make me jealous? Why are you all buddy-buddy with Jay now? Going out and exchanging numbers."

I relax a little, crossing my arms over my bare torso as I watch him. My teeth scrape across my bottom lip briefly as I take in his flustered appearance.

"You seem a little pissed off."

"Don't fuck around with my friends just to get to me."

"You know what, Campbell? Maybe I'm not thinking about you at all. You tell me to leave you alone because you don't want anybody to know what we did, so I say I'll leave you alone. Now I'm talking to other people, and you can't seem to stand it. You think I don't see you watching me every time we're on the field?"

"You're my competition. Of course I'm watching."

I snort. "You think I didn't see the jealousy dripping from your eyes as I was talking to Jay? The hurt on your face when you saw me give him my number? You say you don't want me talking to you, but you don't want me talking to anyone else? I don't think you have that right."

He takes a few seconds to figure out his reply. "I don't want you playing with Jay's feelings. He's into guys and you know that. Don't make him think he has a chance if you're only doing it to make me mad."

I let out a humorless laugh. "You're funny."

"I'm serious, Dominic."

I narrow my eyes at him. "Maybe I like Jay. He's good looking, funny, and charismatic. And you know what else? He's out of the closet. Stop thinking what I'm doing has anything to do with you. You're not interested, right?"

I raise my brows at him, taking a step closer and waiting for his answer. His eyes track my movements, roaming down my face to my chest and abdomen. My towel hangs around my hips just like it did the first time I saw him.

Taking another step, I close the gap between us. "Right? You don't want me? So I can fuck Jay if I want to. He's single. I'm single. You'd be okay with that, wouldn't you? You're not gonna cock block your friend, are you?"

Anger mixed with desire swirls in his eyes as he watches me, his jaw tense as he clenches a fist at his side. I'm not worried he's gonna punch me. I'm thinking he's more concerned with touching me.

"Don't," he says through gritted teeth.

"Don't what?"

"Don't fuck Jay."

He avoids eye contact, touching his chin to his chest as he looks down.

"Why?" I ask. Trevor's chest heaves but he doesn't look at me. I bring my finger to his chin and lift his head until he's looking into my eyes. "Tell me why."

I can read in his expression that he's fighting the urge to tell me the truth. He doesn't want to admit it. He's afraid I'll hold this admission over his head, and maybe I will, but I need to hear it.

"Because I don't want you to."

My lips curl up slightly and my hand slides to his neck, my fingers pressing on the base of his skull while my thumb skates over his cheek. "And why is that?"

He huffs and tries to move his head, but I bring him back and force him to meet my gaze. "Because I—"

A door closing and footsteps approaching forces us apart right before I get his answer.

"Hurry up, guys. It's Friday," Coach says with a grin as he spots us.

"Yes, Coach," Trevor answers, his eyes lingering on me as he makes his getaway.

~

After getting home, I find my mom on the couch, watching TV. Like she said she was gonna do, she cleaned up the house a little bit and based on the slight curl of her hair, she showered today too.

"Hey," I say, sitting next to her.

"Hi, honey. How was your day?"

I shrug. "Fine. How was yours?"

"About the same, I guess."

"Did Ms. Anne come over today?"

"She did. She brought me some food. That was nice."

I nod. "She wants to make sure you're okay."

"I don't really know how to feel, to be honest."

Mom hasn't opened up too much since I've been home. She's aware of my feelings or lack thereof for my father, so she's not surprised by my lack of emotion when it comes to his death. She hasn't asked why I'm not sad or why I haven't cried, just like I haven't asked her why she has.

Before I left for college, we had a fight about him. I yelled at her and asked why she kept us in the same house. I questioned if she cared about me or herself. I said a lot of things I wish I could take back, but I was an angry teenager.

I had been abused, but she's been abused, too. She's probably suffered more than I did, but I thought that would make it easier to leave. However, I know it wouldn't have been easy. She had no money, no job, no family nearby, and probably felt like staying with him was her only choice. I'm sure she loved him in her own way, regardless of how he treated her.

"What do you mean?"

She gives me a tight smile, tilting her head. "I know you and your father didn't get along at the end."

"We never did, Mom."

She nods, looking away. "I'm not a naive woman, Dom. I'm sure you think I'm stupid and selfish for staying when things were bad."

"Mom."

She holds up a hand. "Your father used to be a good man. I know you didn't see a lot of that, but he cared about me. He loved us. I knew him when I was just a girl, and he was the most charming boy I had ever come across. He was outgoing and funny. But life got to him, like it does to many people. Some people succumb to their vices. Alcohol and pills were your father's and he couldn't rip himself from their grip."

"I don't think he deserves to be painted as a victim."

"I'm not saying he was innocent. He could've tried harder and made better decisions."

"Like not hitting us? Yeah, I'd say so."

She takes a breath. "I was devastated at first, and I'm still sad. I grieve for the boy I met and the young man that had so much potential. I grieve for you because you never had the father you deserved. I'm worried about my future, but..." she dabs at her eyes and pulls herself together. "There are times when I wake up or walk in here and feel relief. I no longer have to walk on eggshells or worry what might ignite his rage. And in those moments, I feel guilty."

I reach out and hold her hand in mine. "Don't feel guilty, Mom. Your feelings, all of them, are valid and important. You feel how you feel."

Tears trickle down her cheeks as she looks at me and her chin wobbles. "I'm sorry, Dom. I'm so sorry."

Before I can say anything, she gets up and apologizes once more before rushing to her room.

Hours go by and she doesn't come back out. I'm due to meet up with Jay soon, so I head to her door and knock.

"Mom?"

A few seconds later she replies. "Yeah?"

"Are you okay?"

"I'm fine," she says with a sniffle.

"I was gonna go out, but I can stay here."

"No, no. Go. Have fun. I promise I'm okay."

"You sure?"

"I'm sure. Be safe, okay?"

"Okay." I wait a beat. "I love you."

"I love you, too," she replies in a shaky voice.

Nine

DOMINIC

I END up meeting Jay and a few of his friends in front of the bar.

"You ate, right?" It's the first thing he says when he sees me. When I raise my brows, he continues, "Because we're about to drink our weight in alcohol!"

I laugh. "I ate, but I also drove here."

He cuts his hand through the air. "Don't worry about that. We have a DD." Turning toward the two people to his right, he says, "This is Bryant and Olivia." He gestures to me. "This is Dom."

"You're always making new friends," Olivia says with a smile. "Nice to meet you, Dom."

"You too."

Bryant gives me a once over before lifting his chin and grinning. Definitely gay and definitely checking me out. He's not too bad on the eyes either. Tall and thin, soft looking skin, and someone I could definitely see myself having some fun with.

Jay chuckles, slapping my shoulder as he catches me looking Bryant up and down. "Yeah, yeah. Let's head inside.

The guys will be here soon. Shea texted me that they stopped for food first."

Inside, the place is dark with neon lights flashing from another room, and the lamps hanging above the bar are a mix of red, blue, and green. Loud laughter and cheering filters in from the left, a group of people crowding around something.

"Mechanical bull," Jay says into my ear. "People go crazy for it, but you ain't about to catch me on that thing. Just so you know."

I laugh. "Me neither. I'd just embarrass myself."

"Down to the right is a dance floor. They play a decent mix of music." He struts ahead to the bar, passing the bull on our left. "Whatever you want, they got it. What do you normally drink?"

I don't bother to tell him I hardly drink, but I definitely feel like forgetting some shit tonight, so I say, "Give me whatever you usually get."

He watches me for a second, a smile growing. "You sure?"

"Yeah."

With a laugh, he turns around and gets the bartender's attention, and now I'm starting to wonder what the hell he usually drinks.

Olivia and Bryant stand to our left, placing their orders, and I spin around to check out the room. It's definitely more spacious than I anticipated. Though there's a lot of people here, it doesn't feel crowded. Half the tables are full, but most of the customers are standing. Music blasts, making people sway even if they aren't on the dancefloor.

"Here you go," Jay says, handing me a glass with dark liquid in it and then passing me a shot glass. "We always take shots first."

"What the hell is this?" I ask, inspecting the reddish drink.

"It's Liv's favorite," he replies, shooting her a wink that makes her roll her eyes and smile. "Red-headed slut."

I take in Liv's red hair and wonder if that's why. She shakes her head. "It's not just because of my hair. It's a good drink."

We all clink our glasses together. "To new friends."

After swallowing down the shot and placing the empty glass on the bar top, I take a sip of whatever drink Jay gave me and instantly regret taking such a huge sip.

"What the fuck is this?"

He chokes out a laugh, almost spitting out his drink. "It's Between the Sheets."

"That helps a lot," I deadpan. "I don't know names of drinks."

"It's hennessy, rum, and lemon juice and some other shit. I don't know."

"Good god, man. That's strong."

"I take it you're not used to drinking."

"Nah. Not really."

Bryant takes a sip out of his glass, looking at me with amusement in his eyes. "I learned the hard way, too. Don't let Jay choose your drink. He had me stumbling home the first time we went out. I stick to my fruity, slushy drinks."

"What's that?" I ask.

"Ocean Blue. Pina Colada mix, coconut rum, pineapple juice, and probably splashes of some other stuff."

By the time I've finished most of the drink Jay got me, the football guys show up and want to take another shot. This time it's something called a bomb pop, which is pretty good.

"Tim, you're buying us our next drinks," Jay says.

"Why am I buying you a drink? I only made a bet with Dom."

"Come on, man. Remember when I hooked you up with that one chick?"

They fall into a conversation as they wait for the

bartender, so I walk over to where Bryant and Olivia are sitting.

"Feeling tipsy yet?" Olivia asks.

"Not yet," I answer with a grin. "I'm pretty big. It's gonna take a little more than two shots and one drink to have me drunk."

I don't miss her eyes skating over my biceps and chest, and then I find Bryant chewing on his bottom lip as he watches me.

"Definitely big," she says. "So, what's your story?"

"Is that everyone's go-to question here?" I ask with a laugh.

She shrugs. "Sorry. Nosy, I guess."

"It's fine. I just transferred here from Grand Valley."

She nods, taking a sip of her drink. "Mhm. And are you single, taken, gay, straight, something in between?"

I smile, enjoying her bluntness. "Single and gay."

"Damn. Sucks for me. But Bryant's gay," she says, reaching out to squeeze his wrist.

My eyes flicker to Bryant's pink cheeks. "Thanks, Liv," he murmurs.

"I'm just saying," she says, holding her hands up.

"You and Jay together or something?" I ask.

She tilts her head from side to side like she's thinking. "Sometimes. We hook up from time to time."

"No strings attached."

"Exactly."

Jay and the other guys come over, drinks in hand, and we all move to the room with the dance floor and get drunker and drunker as the hours go by. I end up losing track of how many shots I've had, and I dance with both Olivia and Bryant until Jay pulls her away. Shea and Tim find girls to dance with and buy drinks for, and then at some point we end up next to the damn mechanical bull.

We must've been extremely drunk, because somehow me and Jay both end up on the bull at the same time. We fall almost as soon as they speed it up, but then we get back on and try again.

Once we've failed a couple more times, we leave and watch the rest of our group attempt to hold on while we sit in a nearby booth.

"This is the most fun I've had in a long time," I admit to Jay, yelling over the music and voices.

"Yes! A fucking success. Now I need to get you laid, then I'll have done my job."

I laugh, falling into his side. We're both so wasted, but I don't miss the moment his eyes linger on my lips, and when our glassy eyes meet, it's for a second too long, because I know where this could go.

Though I'm drunk, I'm still aware of Trevor's plea to not hook up with his friend. It's not that I don't find Jay attractive. He definitely is, and I like him a lot, but I know that if we did anything, it would be a one-time thing. Something fun to do because we're drunk. It would lead nowhere, and honestly, I want to see if this thing with Trevor escalates. He's a challenge, and I want to win.

I laugh off our collision and pull away, taking another drink. Jay doesn't take offense. He may not have even been aware that I was conscious of where his thoughts were. He simply laughs with me and then makes fun of Shea who was just thrown from the bull.

Olivia saunters over and sits in his lap, and I'm quickly forgotten as they begin to makeout.

We all stay until closing, which is two in the morning. I'm way too drunk to drive myself home, but true to his word, Jay had a DD figured out and this guy pulled up in a huge SUV and drove all of us home. Getting our cars will be something to figure out with a sober mind, but I'm not too worried about it right now.

I pass out around three and wake up at noon to a million notifications on my phone, but one that surprises me the most is from Trevor.

Ten

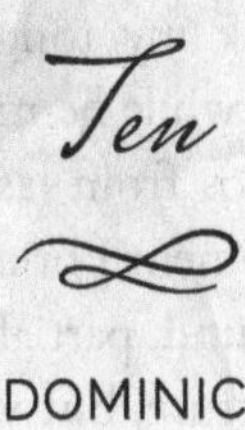

DOMINIC

THE NOTIFICATION from Trevor isn't really from him. It's from Instagram letting me know he followed me. That alone lets me know he doesn't hate me, even if he wants to act like he does.

I don't get on my social media accounts too often, but I manage a post twice a month or so. At first I think he searched me out to follow me, but after opening the app, I find I have over twenty notifications, and considering my last post was over a month ago, it's surprising.

Trevor wasn't the only one who followed me. Jayden, Bryant, and Olivia followed me, as well as several other football guys. As soon as I look over the other notifications, and look at the things I was tagged in, I realize why this is happening. Several people were documenting last night's activities and I'm in a handful of photos and videos—most of which I don't remember even happening.

In a few of Jayden and Olivia's stories, I'm documented in the booth drinking and laughing. In one video that Liv took, it's me and Jayden on that damn bull, and it has me cracking up to watch. Jayden's behind me, holding onto my waist as we laugh before we tumble to the mat below.

Jay posted a couple group shots of all of us holding our shot glasses and making faces. One is of me and him, looking beyond wasted as I stick my tongue out, holding up my pointer and pinky finger while he makes a goofy face. I scroll through everyone's photos from last night and come across one that captured the moment I briefly thought about kissing Jay. We're in the background, partially covered by Shea who's the main focus of the picture, but we're close and looking at each other with curious and lust-filled eyes.

I would bet one million dollars that Trevor's looked through these and is seething.

I follow everyone back and like and comment on a few photos before I finally climb out of bed, shower, and brush my teeth.

Once I'm dressed, I search the house for my mom, and when I don't find her, I walk out to the porch and see her talking to Ms. Anne, so I make my way back in the house and search for some food. We don't have much in here, so I'll have to go to the grocery store.

Grabbing the keys, I jog down the three concrete steps and approach my mom.

"Hey."

"Hey, baby," Mom greets as Anne smiles at me.

"I'm gonna go buy some food. I won't be gone long. Do you want anything specific?"

"I don't think so," she answers. "Oh, whatever these are," she adds, picking up a cookie from the plate that sits between them.

"They're just pecan sandies," Anne says.

"They're addicting," Mom says with a small laugh.

Glad she's eating, even if it is cookies. I plan to buy three packs of them. "Okay. I'll be back in a little while."

"Be careful," she says to my back as I head for the car.

Before I go to the grocery store, I decide to stop at this burger place where you walk up to the window and order. There's no drive-thru, but they're worth getting out for, so I park my car, round the building, and wait in the line.

I pull my phone from my pocket and head back to Instagram to read more comments. Jay already responded to one of mine, asking when we're doing it again. Shea has bet me that the next time we go, he'll outride me on the bull.

I move up a space in line before I notice Trevor. He's sitting at one of the tables with two other guys, and as far as I can tell, he hasn't noticed me yet.

He looks good in his plain white tee and sunglasses pushed up on top of his blond hair. One of the guys says something that makes him laugh. It's a hearty laugh that showcases his teeth and has his head dropping back. As I watch him, I find myself smiling. His laugh and smile are contagious and I hate that I like them so much already.

I have ten minutes to figure out what I want to do. That's how long I'm in line and then waiting for my order to be ready. I debate on whether I want to just take my food to my car to avoid seeing Trevor, or if I should approach him and say hi. I don't want to make him uncomfortable, but I guess I can tone down my flirting and teasing and just say hi like any other person would. I have no intention of outing him to his friends, it's just hard not to check him out.

The lady at the window hands me my food on a tray which settles my debate. It's not in a to-go bag, so I take the tray and walk over to a table and sit down. Yes, it just so happened to be the table next to him.

When I sit, all three sets of eyes turn to see who's next to them, but it's only Trevor's whose stay trained on me.

I smile. "Hey, Campbell."

His eyes flicker to his friends' and then back to me. "Hey."

The guys he's with do a double-take now that he's spoken to me. The one closest to me has dark hair and a sculpted face, while the one to his left has lighter hair and a softer face, but both are pretty attractive.

"Campbell," the dark-haired one says with humor, studying his friend. "I take it you're football buddies. Only athletes do that shit."

Trevor rolls his eyes. "Yeah, he's new." Shifting in his seat, he focuses on dipping a fry in ketchup.

His friend inspects me again. "Trevor's obviously shit at introducing people, so I'll introduce myself. I'm Renzo, and this is my boyfriend Ronan." He rubs the other guy's back. "You are?"

"Dominic, but I usually go by Dom."

He nods, but looks back at Trevor, who's now avoiding even his gaze. Something weird is going on, but I have no idea what it could be.

"You're new?" Renzo asks, his brows furrowed.

"Yeah."

"Did you come from Grand Valley?" he asks.

Two things happen simultaneously. Trevor's head snaps up and Renzo's boyfriend gasps.

My eyes bounce between all of them, trying to read the situation. "Uh, yeah."

There's a few beats of silence and some sort of weird silent conversation happening between them before Ronan stands up, gathering trash.

"Babe, we gotta go. We have to meet Vi and Dex."

Renzo looks at me once more before turning his focus on Trevor, who's looking at him with an unreadable expression. Renzo chuckles and shakes his head, standing up.

"Well, this was fun," he says. "Nice meeting you, Dom."

I grin and nod, and once they're both gone, I watch Trevor visibly relax. His shoulders drop as he exhales.

"Do they know about what we did?" I ask, trying to piece things together. "They know you're gay?"

He sighs. "Yeah, they're the only ones who know."

I get up and move to sit at his table.

Eleven

TREVOR

LAST NIGHT I was in my bed, scrolling through Instagram and seeing picture after picture of Dominic. Dominic who was always within touching distance of Jay—sometimes even pressed against him.

I couldn't even help myself when I clicked that follow button. Stupid late night decisions mixed with jealousy and enough interest that made me want to be able to see what he was up to.

I don't know what the hell I'm gonna do when it comes to Dominic. I hate that I want him as much as I do. I hate how infuriating he is and how no matter how much he gets on my nerves, I still crave to be around him. There's something about him that ropes me in.

Before school even started, I told Renzo and Ronan about my hookup with a nameless man in a bathroom. It was the next day when I spilled my guts to them, because they're the only ones who know about me.

Of course, Renzo gave me shit for another drunken bathroom hookup, considering what happened between us. But that's another story. We've moved on from that, and he and

Ronan both understand what I'm going through. Ronan mostly, since he was just in my shoes not too long ago.

When I told them about the bathroom blowjob, I didn't expect the guy to show up to South River. I hate that I told them it happened at Grand Valley, because if I had kept that to myself, Renzo wouldn't have put together that Dom is who I hooked up with. Now I'll expect a call from him later asking why I didn't tell him that the guy moved here.

For now, I focus on my food and do my best to ignore the sexy man that sits across from me, asking questions. If I look into his dark eyes, I'll get lost in them. If I study the prominent peaks of his upper lip that form the perfect cupid's bow, I'll want to kiss them. If I focus on the dark scruff on his angular jaw, I'll want to feel the scratch of it against my skin.

"How did they find out?" he asks.

I sigh and look up to the sky, not really wanting to have this conversation. "It's a long story."

"Lucky for me I don't have anywhere to be for a while."

I shake my head. "You're insufferable, you know that?"

He smirks. "You like that I bother you."

"Why would I like that?"

"You tell me," he says with all the confidence in the world.

He's not wrong, but I don't know why I like his annoying ass so much.

"Anyway, I hooked up with Renzo once. After that he met his now boyfriend, and at the time Ronan wasn't out either. He ended up confessing to me that he liked Renzo, and we talked about our shared closetedness. Ronan eventually came out, but they're the only ones that know."

"So two of your friends are gay, and Jayden is bi, and you're still afraid people will care that you like cock?"

I huff. "It's not just about my closest friends. I don't think they'll care, but I don't know about everyone else. Like the guys on the team, other friends and classmates. My family. It's not easy for everyone. Let me guess, your parents know about you and love you anyway?"

His jaw clenches. "You don't know shit about my family, Campbell, or what I've been through."

"And you don't know what coming out might have me go through."

He gives a quick nod as he takes a sip out of his straw. "Touché."

We sit in silence for a few minutes, eating our food and looking anywhere but at each other. I finally speak up.

"So, you had fun last night."

Not a question. I can tell from the videos and pictures that he did.

His lips turn up on the ends. "I did. I'm assuming you saw all the posts."

"Yeah." I don't bring up him and Jay because it's not really my place, and I don't want him to know how bothered I am by the idea of them getting close.

"Yeah, Jay's pretty cool. So are his friends Olivia and Bryant."

"You met Bryant?" I ask.

He nods. "He was checking me out."

I shake my head and snort. "Of course."

"I'm assuming you know he's gay, too? Something in the water around here or what?"

I laugh at that, and his twinkling eyes meet mine as he smiles.

We stare at each other too long, because I'm already envisioning all the things I want us to do together. He knows where my mind goes, because his carefree smile falls and his tongue swipes across his bottom lip as his eyes flicker from my eyes to my mouth and back up again.

"You can pretend you hate me all you want, but I think we both know where we're gonna end up eventually."

"Where's that?" I ask, my voice airer than I want it to be.

He leans in and drops his voice. "You on your knees with my cock in your mouth. Followed by you on your knees as I sink into you."

Warmth floods my cheeks and my pulse ticks up.

"You like that idea, don't you?" he asks, voice gravelly.

"I don't...I...you. Umm." I shake my head, unable to voice my thoughts.

How can I tell him I haven't thought too much about what it would be like to have a dick in my ass, let alone his massive one. The thought scares me while also sparking curiosity. I want to know what that would feel like.

His hand moves like he's about to reach out and touch me, but then he remembers where we are and pulls it back, and I know it was done for me.

"Fuck. The things I'd do to you. You're just denying yourself something you'd enjoy."

"How would I know if I'd enjoy it?"

He inhales deeply, a low rumble in his throat. "I can't tell you how much I love how innocent and new you are."

Once more I feel heat bloom in my cheeks.

"You'd enjoy it, Trevor. You'd enjoy everything I'd do to you. You remember how you got off from my hand, don't you? Imagine my tongue dancing around the head of your cock. Imagine me licking you in places you've never thought to expose to someone."

My dick comes to life as images flash in my head and my hand drops to my lap.

He grins, victorious.

Right before I'm about to give in and beg him to come to my house and do all the filthy things he wants to me, he stands up.

"You think about that. Let me know." He's so casual

about it, like it's a game to him. Like he's not as affected as I am.

I open my mouth, gazing up at him in confusion. "You're leaving?"

"Yeah. I have to go to the store before I go to work." I don't know what to say, so I say nothing. He gathers his trash and looks down at me. "You know how to contact me if you want me."

"Want you?" I say stupidly.

He grins. "I'm not gonna beg to fuck you, Campbell. I've let you know where I stand. You want me? Tell me you do."

"You want me to beg you?" I question.

His teeth sink into his bottom lip. "Mm. That might be nice."

As he's walking to the trash can, I yell, "That's not gonna happen!"

I hear him laugh, but he doesn't turn around. He lifts a hand and gives me a peace sign. God, I've never hated someone so much and yet wanted to fuck them more than I wanted my next breath.

Twelve

TREVOR

"**BEG**," I say out loud, scoffing at the idea.

He's clearly out of his mind. How does he switch so easily like that? One second he's saying all these filthy things, describing what he'd do to me, and the next, he's casually walking off like it wasn't a big deal.

I haven't stopped thinking about it since I saw him earlier this afternoon, and I regret not leaving when he came to sit with me.

When he's around, something weird happens. It's like he brings with him this bubble, and when he's close, I get trapped inside and it changes everything I thought I knew about myself. I'm not the type to be so meek and easily controlled. But like the time in the bathroom, and the times in the locker room, he gets close to me, and I'm sucking on his finger, choking on his cock, and nearly begging for more. I'm entranced by his confidence. He tells me to get on my knees, and I'm already halfway there. What the fuck?

On the flip side, he aggravates the shit out of me. The same confidence I enjoy when I'm trapped in his bubble, turns into annoying cocky behavior outside of that bubble.

Everything in me is fighting to stay strong and not surrender to his will. Even being with him at Bobby's Burgers was hard. If anybody was paying attention to us, they would've known, or at least suspected something was going on between us. That's one of the main reasons why I don't want to be around him. My wall comes down too easily and I'll end up outing myself by accident.

I park in my driveway, and just as I'm about to call Jay back, my phone vibrates in my hand, and Renzo's face pops up on the screen. Knowing I'm in for a long conversation, I plop down on the top step of my porch.

"Don't start," I say as soon as I accept the call.

He laughs. "So, Dom is the towel wrapped hottie from Grand Valley? And he's here now and playing football with you? And, more importantly, you didn't fucking tell me?"

I sigh. "It's not gonna be a thing. There's no need to know he transferred here."

"Right, except that he's fucking hot, and when you saw him earlier, your jaw dropped like you were ready to swallow his dick right at the table. Which I'm not one-hundred percent against seeing, if I'm being honest."

I shake my head, a laugh escaping even though I was trying to keep it in. "I'm assuming Ronan isn't around."

"He's in the other room," he answers easily. "He agrees he's hot, and we both agree that you're gonna hook up with him again. You'd be stupid not to."

I groan. "You're supposed to be my friend and on my side."

"I am, and I'm being a great friend by saying you need to get laid by the massive football player. You'd feel better, I promise. You have so much pent up...what's the word I'm looking for?"

"Sexual energy?" Ronan chirps in the background.

"Sexual energy works," Renzo says. "You haven't had sex with a guy yet. You're craving it. I know it."

"Oh my God, I'm not talking about this with you."

Renzo laughs again. "Anyway, why aren't y'all doing anything?"

"For one, I'm in the closet."

"And? So was Ronan. We had a blast hooking up behind people's backs."

I roll my eyes and push my sunglasses up on my head. "When I'm around him, my guard comes down, and I don't want people figuring it out because I'm eye-fucking him. Plus, I don't even know how to go about telling people. Everyone I know has always thought I was straight my whole life. Hell, I was hooking up with chicks this year. How will I explain my revelation?"

"Say that you hooked up with *thee* Lorenzo Hayes and realized how much you loved dick." Only a second goes by before he exclaims, "Ow. Sorry, babe."

"Ronan's gonna kick your ass."

"Kiss it, more like. Anyway, who cares what they think?"

"I don't know how to tell my parents."

"Your parents have always been pretty cool, and they like me and know I'm gay, so..."

"Yeah, but you're not their son. It's easy to pretend you tolerate something when it doesn't involve your kid."

"Have they ever talked about me when I wasn't around? Judged my sexuality?"

"No," I answer honestly.

"I know it's scary, but you don't want to miss out on opportunities because you're scared."

"What opportunities?"

"Uhh, to bang the hot football player? I thought I was clear."

"Renzo," I hear Ronan say in the background.

"Okay, that's just one thing, but to be serious, the opportunity to be yourself. To break free from the shackles of what society thinks we all need to be. You deserve the opportunity to be happy with whoever brings you that happiness, regardless of what's between their legs."

"Thanks."

"No problem. You know you'll always have us even if all your other friends turn out to be pieces of shit."

I laugh. "I appreciate that. I gotta call Jay back, so I'll hit you up later."

"All right, man."

I end the call, head inside, and call Jay.

"Hey, man," he answers right away.

"Hey."

"So, I feel kinda bad for leaving you out of last night's festivities, because it was a pretty fun fucking night."

I snort. "Thanks."

"So, I was thinking we could go out tonight."

"You know I'm not twenty-one for another month. Why don't we have a party here?"

"How about both?"

I groan. "You want to go to that lame ass bar?"

"It's the only place that allows eighteen and up in."

"Yeah, and I have to wear a bright green wristband to alert everyone I'm underage."

Jayden laughs. "It's not that bad. Wear a long sleeve shirt. And the bar isn't that lame."

"You literally called it the shittiest bar in America."

"Maybe I was exaggerating. It's not like I've been to every bar in America."

I run a hand through my hair. "Ugh, fine. But I don't want to stay too long. We'll drink a little and then come back here. I don't even know why we go out when we can drink in the comfort of our own homes."

"It's called socializing, Trev. We might make new friends."

"Don't you have enough friends?" I grumble.

"No, and you definitely need more."

"Fine. When?"

"Ten?"

"All right."

I end the call and realize I have several hours before then, so the plan is to do some homework, call my parents, take a nap, eat, shower, and get ready to go.

I briefly wonder if telling my parents I'm gay over the phone is acceptable. Definitely seems easier. Problem is, they live nearby, so it's not like I have a good excuse. Mom would be over in a heartbeat.

We moved here from West Virginia when I was twelve. I love this part of Michigan, and South River is top notch, so I never felt the need to leave the state to go to college. My relationship with my parents isn't bad either, but I still have this overwhelming sense of dread weighing heavy on me at the thought of telling them.

Maybe when I call, I'll make plans to go over and visit next weekend, and I can tell them then. It gives me a week to figure out how to go about it.

Yeah. That's the plan. One week. Then I can figure out this thing with Dominic.

Thirteen

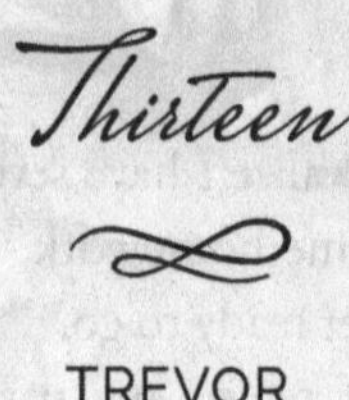

TREVOR

"KNOCK, KNOCK," Jayden says right before bursting through my front door.

I finish sliding my wallet into my pocket. "You sure we have to go to this bar?"

"You should really lock your door," he says, ignoring me as he walks to my kitchen. "I could've been anybody."

I swipe my phone off the counter and pocket that as well. "I knew you were coming over. Plus, it's a pretty safe neighborhood."

"Pft, you're telling me. Your neighbors are all retired folks." He pulls a bottle of Jack Daniels out of my cabinet followed by two shot glasses.

"My parents got me this place," I say, watching him pour the amber liquid.

"Yeah, apparently they thought if you lived in a retirement community you wouldn't get in trouble. But look at you, drinking before it's legal," he says with a grin, handing me a glass.

I make a face. "It's not a retirement community."

Jayden snorts. "At least they don't call the cops on you for having parties."

"Probably because they're asleep at eight o'clock."

We both laugh and then down the shots after clinking our glasses.

"All right. Uber should be here soon, because I am not gonna be a DD and I don't have one lined up."

"Dude, you know I'm not gonna be able to drink over there. I can obviously drive us back."

"But I'm gonna slip you shots, because it's my duty to get you fucked up."

I shake my head and laugh. "You're terrible. I'll just get drunk when we come back here."

"Well, I already ordered the car, so there's that." He looks out the window. "And they pulled up. Let's go."

It's nearing ten-thirty when we get to the bar, and we spot Bryant and Olivia walking up to the door just as we pull up.

"Hey, perfect timing," Liv says with a huge smile. "We missed you last night."

"Yeah, yeah. Don't lie to me."

She smacks my shoulder. "Look, there may not be a bull to ride in here, but we're still gonna have a good time."

"I'm not even trying to be here that long, but Jayden wouldn't take no for an answer," I say, jerking my head in his direction.

"Yeah, he's just used to getting his way."

Jay rolls his eyes. "Come on, Bryant. Let's leave these two behind."

Inside, the bar is playing some Nirvana while a handful of people in their forties or fifties sit at the bar. It's a fairly small place, but it's well-kept. The guy at the door was sure to slap a neon band around my wrist after checking IDs, but just to make sure I don't cut it off or cover it up, I also got a huge black X on my hand in Sharpie.

Me and Liv find a booth while Bryant and Jay go up and order drinks. Besides the people at the bar, there's three other booths full of people. Two of the tables look like they're probably in their thirties, and the other table has a couple underage girls, based on the neon bands.

Thirty minutes later, Renzo, Ronan, Dex, and Violet all come in, and our one table quickly grows to three. Thanks to the huge group of people surrounding our booth, I'm able to sneakily take a shot without any employees seeing.

When I hear a chorus of "Heys!" ring out, I look around, wondering who else showed up, and my gaze locks onto Dominic.

"You work here, dude?" Tim asks him.

"Did the shirt not give it away?" he asks with a laugh.

"Aw man, we're all here getting drunk, and you have to work," Shea says.

Dom laughs, not yet seeing me. "It's fine. I had way too much fun yesterday."

"When are you off?" Jay asks.

Oh no. I know where this is going.

"One, maybe a little before. Why?" he asks, clearing a table nearby.

"We're heading to Trev's house when we're done here. You should come."

At the mention of my name, his head swivels until he finds me. His lips twitch briefly as he studies me, like he's trying to hold back a grin.

"Yeah, that might be fun." His eyes twinkle with mischief. "Give me the address and I'll be there."

When I finally tear my eyes away from him and the way

the tight black shirt stretches across his chest and biceps, I find an amused Renzo staring at me.

"Don't."

He laughs, draping an arm around Ronan's shoulders. "I didn't say anything."

Knowing Dominic is gonna be at my house tonight, I start sneaking sips out of Jay and Ronan's drinks, hoping it'll calm my racing heart. Instead, all it does is make me anxious to get home. I find I want him there, in my space. I begin imagining ways we can sneak off and have a moment alone, and that's exactly what I shouldn't be thinking about.

I'll have a house full of my friends, and any one of them could catch us. Hell, they might notice how I can't stop looking at him. Hopefully they'll be too drunk and preoccupied to worry about me.

"Thinking of having a sleepover tonight?" Renzo asks me, leaning into my side.

"Shut up."

He chuckles and surprisingly doesn't say anything else.

"We ready to go?" Jay announces. "This place just had last call, so they're gonna be closing soon."

"Yeah, let me take a piss first."

"Cool. I'm getting an Uber."

"I'm sober, so I can drive some of y'all over," Vi says.

I walk away from the table and across the bar, heading toward the bathrooms on the opposite end.

As I'm about to push the door, it opens up and I come face to face with Dominic.

When he realizes it's me, he gestures for me to come in while wearing his signature cocky smirk. "Well, hello. We seem to have a thing for bathrooms."

I roll my eyes and move past him. "I wouldn't say that."

"No?" he asks, following me inside. "Should we discuss how we first met?"

I ignore him, walking to a urinal and undoing my jeans.

"Or what about the times in the locker room? That's basically an oversized bathroom."

"We didn't do anything in the locker room."

"You didn't suck on my thumb while looking up at me with sex-filled eyes, desperate for more?"

I hate him. I fucking hate him. He's right, but I hate that he's right.

"And here we are. What could we do in here? Your dick is already out."

I angle my head over my shoulder. "I'm taking a piss. Do you want me to pee on you?"

He crosses his arms over his chest and gives a slight shrug. "Not really my kink."

"What is?" I ask before thinking better of it.

"You can find out."

Warmth floods my cheeks, so I quickly finish up and walk to the sink. "So, I guess you're coming to my house."

"Don't sound too excited."

I shut off the water and turn around to walk to the hand dryer, which he is standing right next to. "I really don't care," I say, hoping it's believable.

He grins like he can see right through me. "Okay."

I shake my head, letting out a huff. "You're really fucking annoying."

"I don't think I'm annoying. I think you want me. You want me so bad it hurts. You like that I've taken an interest in you. You enjoy that I flirt with you even though you say you hate it. If I stopped paying attention to you, you'd be upset. You want me to want you, but you won't allow yourself to admit you want me. You want to be able to act out every single thing you've thought about doing to me, but you're afraid. You're scared to want me. You hate that you actually like me, and that's what's annoying. Not me."

I stare at him, stuck in place. He's right. Of course he fucking is, and of course I fucking hate it. I'm not about to admit that to him, though.

Dominic pushes away from the wall and steps up to me, his foot touching mine. "You already know I want you, and you know that *I* know you want me." His nose barely grazes my cheek as his breath dances across my skin. "Just admit it, Campbell. I won't tell anyone. Tell me you want me and let me give it to you." His lips touch the shell of my ear, and at this moment I'm trapped in his bubble. I'm ready to tell him whatever he wants to hear just so he'll touch me. My body aches for his touch.

A laugh outside the door bursts the bubble right before it swings open. My heart hammers in my chest at the thought of getting caught being so close to Dominic. Thank God it's only Renzo.

He takes in the scene and grins. "Hey, boys." His eyes find mine. "Cars are ready to go. Waiting on you."

"Yeah, okay. I'm coming."

"Looks like I walked in before that could happen," he jokes. "Sorry."

Dom chuckles, unaffected.

I throw Renzo a look, but he just shrugs. "See you there?" he asks Dominic.

I look back at him, waiting for his answer. "If Campbell wants me there."

Fucking asshole. He knows what he's doing.

Both Renzo and Dom's gazes are on me, waiting.

"Yeah," I finally say. "Yeah, I want you there."

Dom smiles before I turn and walk out of the bathroom.

Fourteen

TREVOR

AS SOON AS I get home, me and everybody else that was with us at the bar, take a shot. I turn up some music, pull out the alcohol I've collected from people bringing stuff over when I have parties, and tell everyone to make themselves at home.

My place isn't ever really a mess, but now that I know Dominic is coming, I find myself searching every square inch to make sure it looks decent. I head to the bathroom to make sure it's clean, then stop in my room to look over the bed.

Why am I even doing this? Why am I assuming he'll see my bedroom?

I shake my head and march back to the living room. He's just another guy.

"So, I hear you're looking forward to a certain someone showing up," an inebriated Ronan says when I enter the kitchen.

I glare at Renzo who pulls Ronan into his side and kisses his temple. "I tell him everything."

I roll my eyes and glance around to make sure nobody else

is paying attention. "What do you want me to say? Yeah, he's hot." I barely whisper the last two words.

"And you like him," Renzo says.

"I wouldn't say that," I mumble, reaching around him and into the fridge.

"Ooh, is this hate fucking?" Ronan asks.

Renzo chuckles. "Not sure they've even gotten that far yet."

"I really hate that you two know about this."

"Nah, you need us," Renzo says. "We're your only outlet. Look, I know I give you a hard time, but if you like him." I pin him with a look. "Or think he's hot," he amends, rolling his eyes. "Then just do whatever you wanna do. But watch the eye-fucking. It's easy to notice."

I groan. "Yeah, yeah."

"Dom's on his way," Jay says, popping over my shoulder. "He just texted me."

Renzo meets my gaze before his eyes bounce to Jay and back. "Y'all are friends, too?"

Jay laughs. "Too? I'd hardly say Trev has even been nice to the guy," he jokes, bumping my arm. "I told him not to worry about him taking his spot on the team. But anyway, Dom's cool. Nice to look at, too, yeah?" he says with a wide grin and a wink before walking off.

Ronan and Renzo wear matching expressions as they look at me—brows raised, lips slightly parted. Renzo speaks up first.

"Um, do I really need to say it?"

"What?" I ask, annoyance creeping into my tone.

"Jay and Dom could totally hit it off. You know Jay's flirtatious and to the point. If he doesn't know you're into this guy, he could make a move."

My eyes find Jay who's resting his arm on Bryant's shoulder as he talks to Shea and Liv. All eyes are glued to him, everyone entranced by whatever he's saying. He has that way about him. People love being around Jay. He's just a positive and good-hearted person. I have no doubt Dom could be into him.

"I'm not worried about it right now."

"Who's the new guy," Violet says as she pushes her way between us to get to the fridge.

We all look toward the door and I find Dex and Jayden talking to Dom. Renzo looks like he doesn't know what to say, which is weird for him. He's always running his mouth.

"That's Dominic," I answer. "He transferred from Grand Valley."

"Oh, football player? I mean, he has the size," she says, holding a beer.

Renzo gazes down at his sister. "You're drinking that?"

She makes a face. "No, it's for Dex."

"Yeah, he's on the team," I tell her.

"He's hot."

"Yeah," me, Ronan, and Renzo all say at the same time.

I don't even realize my slip until I notice three pairs of wide eyes staring at me. "I mean, what?"

Renzo shakes his head and looks down at Violet, who looks a little sheepish. Everyone is quiet and awkward, then it hits me.

"Do you know?"

She puts her hand on her chest. "I do know, but I swear I haven't told anyone. Not even Dex. Zo told me a while back, before he and Ronan were even together."

"Ah," I say. "The infamous drunken hookup."

Violet bites down on her lip.

Renzo actually looks like he feels bad. "I'm sorry, bro."

I shrug. "It's fine."

Violet touches my arm. "My lips are sealed."

I smile at her. "Thanks."

She moves past us, taking the beer to Dex and introducing herself to Dominic.

"Let's go play whatever they're playing over there," Ronan says, gesturing to the dining room table.

As I walk over, I catch Dominic's gaze. He doesn't look away from me as Jay talks to him, but I eventually break the eye-contact, aware now of the eye-fucking problem I have.

After finishing the game of chandelier, which is just another version of beer pong, some of us start munching on chips while a couple guys jump on the Playstation and play Madden. Someone announces a game of king's cup, and it's not until then that I notice more people are here. Some of the football guys invited some girls over, and there are a couple other guys who are probably just friends of friends.

I've done a pretty good job of ignoring Dominic, even though it's the last thing I want to do. The alcohol in my system has me feeling brave, horny, and stupid. I want to call him to my bedroom, regardless of who's here.

I watch over the top of my cup as he laughs with Jay, and all I can think about are Renzo's words. *Those two could hit it off.*

I down the rest of my drink and find myself talking to Liv and her friend, Naomi. Naomi's a petite brunette who flirts with me instantly. She's cute, and obviously not my type, but I go with it. I flirt back, smiling and making her laugh with stupid jokes. Liv eventually leaves us alone, and she starts touching my arm as she asks me about myself.

She seems like a nice girl, but I have zero interest in doing anything with her. It's just what I should do, right? People might think it's weird if I'm not trying to talk to any of the girls here and instead brood in the corner, staring at the hot new running back.

And just like that, as if he knew I was thinking about him,

Dominic appears, walking up behind Naomi, his eyes trained on me.

She notices when my gaze moves over her head, and turns around and spots Dom. He grins at her. "Can I talk to him for a minute?" he asks.

"Oh." She looks surprised, her eyes finding mine. "Uhh."

"What do you need?" I ask him.

He puts one hand in his pocket while his finger rubs his bottom lip, his piercing gaze pinning me in place. I can tell he's mulling over his thoughts and trying to decide what he wants to say. I probably should've just let her leave us, because now I'm afraid of what he might say.

"Did you hook up with somebody up at Grand Valley? You look familiar."

I clench my jaw and his lips twitch, fighting a grin.

"If I did, it wasn't too memorable."

He laughs then, his eyes going to the floor briefly before he looks back up at me and wets his lips. "Interesting."

I glance at Naomi, who's watching us with confusion marring her face. I have to turn this around.

"Why? Was it your girlfriend or something?"

Dominic chuckles and Naomi finally excuses herself, worried she's about to get caught up in a fight over some chick that doesn't exist.

"Real funny," I say once she's gone. "What's wrong? Jealous?"

"Jealous? Of a woman?" He shakes his head. "Nah. I don't need to be jealous of someone who does nothing for you."

"How do you know? I could fuck her if I wanted to."

His lips pull up on one end and I hate how it highlights his dimple. "Sure," he says with a shrug. "You'd just be thinking about me in order to keep your dick hard."

I take a breath. "You're not the only guy in the world."

He shifts his stance. "Oh, and how many guys have you been with? Because based on your over excitement the first time I touched you, I'd say not many."

My face burns with fury and I imagine what it would be like to punch him in the face. Before I can act on it, I notice Jay making his way over. Dominic must be aware too, because he quickly switches subjects.

"Nice place, man. Not many college kids live in actual houses."

Jay jumps right in the conversation. "Rich kids do. His parents own the house and rent it to him for a good price."

I still feel too mad to fake being nice. Dom just gives me a grin. "Rich boy, huh?"

"To be fair, a lot of people around here are well off," Jay adds. "My family does pretty decent too, but I think I'm the only one out of our close-knit crew who didn't actually grow up here."

"I'm gonna take a piss," I say before walking away.

I end up going to my room and trying to tamp down my frustration. I shouldn't allow him to fuck up my whole mood, but God he's infuriating.

I'm not sure how long I'm gone for, but when I get back to the living room, it's cleared out some. Dex and Violet wave as they walk through the door, and I spot Jay, Zo, and Ronan in the living room, watching two other guys finish their game on the Playstation.

Dominic sits on my couch, his arms spread across the back, eyes on me.

"Hey, we're heading out," Renzo says. "Got an Uber coming."

"Oh, all right."

"You good?" he asks quietly.

"Yeah."

"Maybe there's some hate-fucking that needs to happen,"

he whispers. "I caught a glimpse of some tension earlier. Jesus."

I shake my head. "He's annoying."

He smiles. "Okay, well, have fun."

Him and Ronan say bye to everyone, then Jay walks over to me. "Hey, I'm meeting someone in like twenty minutes," he says, looking at his watch. "Need me to come back tomorrow to help clean up?"

I wave him off. "It's okay. It's not too bad."

He points at Dominic. "You need a ride? I'm heading back toward campus. Where do you stay?"

Dom stands up. "Nah, I'm good. I didn't drink, and I got my car," he says, pulling his keys out.

"Cool. See y'all later," Jay says.

The guys on the Playstation—Shea and Deshawn, finish their game and say their goodbyes, letting me know they're walking down to the twenty-four hour diner a couple blocks away.

And now it's me and Dominic. He swings his keys around his finger, watching me. I'm still annoyed with him, but I also don't want him to leave.

"You said you wanted me here and then did your best to pretend I wasn't," he says. "You start flirting with girls you have no interest in, because that's your M.O., right? Do the exact opposite of what you want to do."

"You don't fucking know me, Dominic. I tell you what I did one time, and now it's my M.O.? Fuck off. You don't know what it's like to be in my shoes."

"Oh, to be the popular rich kid who lives in a three bedroom house before he's twenty-one? To have gay and bi friends but is still too afraid to come out? To want dick but be too much of a pussy to act on it? No, I don't know what that's like."

My resolve snaps, and I rush forward, shoving him back.

He stumbles, but rights himself, standing taller than me by a few inches. "What do you wanna do, Campbell?" he asks, chest heaving. "You wanna fight me?"

He crowds me, bringing his body closer to mine while his head angles downward to study my face. I take a step back, my fists balled at my sides. His hand shoots out and grabs my throat, forcing me to look at him.

"Or do you wanna fuck?"

His large hand squeezes my throat but his eyes are full of desire. He has no intention of fighting me. I know what he wants. I want it too.

I don't say anything, I just press my lips to his in a viscous kiss.

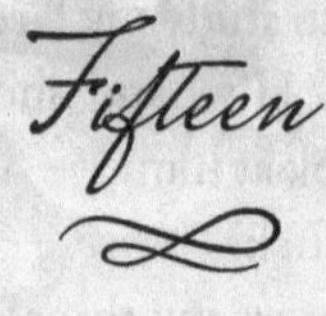

TREVOR

HE DOESN'T SAY ANYTHING. Words aren't needed right now. Our bodies do the talking. He grasps the back of my head with one hand while the other cups my ass, bringing me as close to him as possible. I have one hand on his neck while the other digs into his back. Our cocks grind against each other through the confines of our jeans.

Dominic bites my lip, and I let loose a growl before I thrust my tongue back into this mouth, forcing him to taste the blood he's drawn.

His hand moves to my hair, tugging hard on the strands until he separates us. "Let's go to your room."

I lick the wound on my lip before spinning around and hurrying down the hall with him on my tail. Once inside, before I even have a chance to turn around, Dominic shoves me onto the bed and I land on my stomach.

"Hey," I start to protest.

He lowers his body onto mine and his mouth touches the nape of my neck, planting a soft kiss there before he gets on his knees and tries pulling my shirt off.

I help him out, adjusting my position so I can rip the shirt off and toss it away. He gets off the bed and says, "Turn over."

I do it, watching him undress. His eyes never leave mine and my erection grows painfully hard as he takes his time removing his shirt and undoing his pants.

His body is perfect—someone who is clearly very disciplined in his workout routine and diet. Yeah, a lot of the guys on the team have good bodies, but his is unreal. His shoulders are wide and thick, his chest full, and yet his waist still trim and stomach hard with muscles.

"Undress," he tells me, his boxer-briefs still on, but leaving very little to the imagination.

I kick off my shoes and shove my pants down to my ankles where he reaches down and rips them off.

"Come here," he commands, rubbing a hand over his erection.

I sit up and scoot to the foot of the bed, planting my feet on the floor on either side of his. He gently runs his fingers through my hair before he forces my head back, bringing his thumb to my lips.

"I want you to suck me off."

I'm ready to nod and open my mouth, so fucking needy for his cock. I almost hate myself for how much I want him. For how desperate I am to touch him.

"But I'm not sure you deserve to."

His hand dips into this underwear, and he strokes himself, his crown peeking out from behind the waistband.

I lick my lips.

"You spent all night ignoring me, avoiding me, and then trying to make me jealous."

He pushes his boxer-briefs down to mid-thigh, allowing his erection to spring free right in front of me, but inches from my mouth. Dominic touches himself, teasing me.

"I thought you weren't jealous," I say, finally looking away from his thick cock and into his eyes.

"I said you were trying to make me jealous, not that you succeeded."

He moves a little closer, his hand cupping my cheek while his other hand strokes his length. The crown of his cock is so close to my mouth and it glistens with pre-cum. I lick my lips, anxious to taste him, but he keeps himself just out of reach.

I lean forward, but he moves back. I go to palm my erection, but he slaps my arm away.

"No. We don't want you to get too excited." I narrow my eyes at him. "When you come this time, I want it to be in my mouth."

I bite my lip, dropping my head back. "Jesus Christ."

He brings my head back up, running the tip of his dick across my lips, coating them with his arousal. I've never been so turned on. My cock throbs and my heart thumps rapidly in my chest as fire courses through my veins.

"Open wide."

I do as he says, parting my lips, ready to take him into my mouth.

"Look at me when you taste me."

My stomach clenches with desire and I meet his heated gaze.

"Good boy."

I groan as he shoves his cock across my tongue, my lips stretching around his thickness.

"Ah, yeah," he moans, dipping his dick in and out of my mouth.

My hands move to his ass, squeezing the muscled flesh as he rocks his hips back and forth. He ravishes my mouth with his monstrous size while also gently caressing my head. It's such a weird combination but I love every second of it.

I bring a hand to the base of his erection, stroking him while swirling my tongue around his crown.

"Look at me," he says, his voice deep and husky.

My eyes flicker up at him as my lips close around his cockhead. He takes himself in his hand, so I release my grip on him. He pushes his dick deep into my mouth, trying to reach the back of my throat. When I gag, he eases back.

"Open," he pants. "Tongue out."

I part my lips, my tongue out and waiting. He slaps his cock on it, giving it a few strokes before hitting my tongue with it again. "You like that, don't you?"

I moan, reaching for my dick, needing some sort of friction.

His eyes don't miss my action, and he steps back, denying me any part of him. "Dominic." It's a desperate whispered plea, and one he enjoys based on the smirk on his face.

He pulls me to my feet and shoves my underwear down, so I step out of them, and our dicks touch.

"Fuck," I breathe, looking down at us.

Dominic reaches down and wraps his fingers around my erection, giving me two slow strokes. "Lay down," he whispers against my lips.

Once I'm on my back, Dominic settles himself between my legs, and without any words, lowers his mouth to my cock.

A gasp is snatched from my lungs, like someone reached down my throat and forcefully grabbed my last breath. His mouth is warm and wet, and he sucks me deep into his throat.

After a few minutes of the most intense pleasure I've ever experienced, he pulls off my cock, but his lips and tongue travel up and down my length, kissing and licking every inch of me. I go to put my hands on his head, but change my mind at the last minute and slam them on the bed, gripping the covers.

His lips brush against my balls, and he kisses and licks my sac, before sucking them into his mouth, one at a time.

"Holy shit," I breathe, my hands flying to my head, like I'm trying to keep it from exploding.

His tongue carves a path from under my balls, down my taint, and barely touches my asshole before I'm jerking and jolting.

"Oh God."

He places his hand on my stomach, telling me to relax, and gently licks the area again before dragging his tongue up my shaft again, enclosing me into the warmth of his mouth once more.

"Jesus Christ. I can't take it," I pant, feeling out of my mind with bliss.

He stops what he's doing and grabs my legs, moving me to the side as he says, "Get on your hands and knees."

My heart stutters in my chest. Is he gonna fuck me?

I do as he says, but I manage to get words out this time. "Uh, I don't…"

"I'm not gonna fuck you," he says instantly. "Not tonight anyway, but you're gonna imagine what it'll be like."

He grabs a hold of my hips and slides his cock between my ass cheeks. We both moan at the same time.

"I can't wait to fuck you like this," he says, moving slowly. "You're not gonna be able to walk or sit without thinking about me."

He doesn't need to know I hardly go a minute without thinking about him now. He spits on his cock, but I feel a trickle of the saliva drip between my cheeks, and I don't hate it. He's lubed us up enough to where his cock slides between my cheeks easily.

"Fuck, Campbell," he groans. "Are you leaking for me?"

I feel him shift, and the scruff on his face brushes against my back.

I touch my cock, smearing the pre-cum over my crown. "Yeah," I pant.

"Mm." His body weight is gone, and then he says, "Put your mouth on me. Suck my cock until I shoot my load down your throat, then you can do the same to me."

I turn around and lower my body until I can take him in my mouth. This position has my ass up as he rests on his knees, so while I give him a blowjob, his hand caresses and squeezes my ass.

It's not too much longer before his fingers grip the strands of my hair and he rocks into my mouth, seeking his release. I relax my jaw as much as possible and allow him to fuck me as hard and deep as he can without me choking. I gag once but don't move and definitely don't stop.

He can't move as easily in this position, so he pulls me by my hair until his cock falls from my mouth. He grunts, "lay down," as he guides me toward the pillows.

Slightly propped up, he straddles my chest, his hands on the headboard as he fucks my mouth. I wish I had a video camera in this room, just so I could watch this scene over and over from all angles, because from where I am, this is the hottest fucking thing to ever happen.

Watching his body rock back and forth as he gazes down at his dick disappearing into my mouth makes my own erection throb in anticipation. I touch his ass, thighs, and any other part I can get to.

"Shit," he grunts out, his muscles flexing as he moves faster. "Oh fuck."

He roars as he comes, his cum landing on the back of my tongue and sliding down my throat. I moan and mumble around his dick, trying to swallow and breath at the same time.

Once he's done, he moves down my body and grabs my jaw in his hand, his eyes piercing mine for a few long seconds before he presses his lips to mine, kissing me like hates that he couldn't keep from doing it.

Before I can really even kiss him back, he's gone, his hand on my cock, stroking while his lips close around my crown.

In perfect synchronization, his hand and mouth bring me to the height of arousal in no time. I've been teased to the edge and back a couple times already, so when I glance down and meet his gaze as his tongue circles my head, sliding over my slit, I throw my head back and cry out as I come.

He makes the sexiest noise as he tastes my arousal, and once my body goes limp, he crawls up my body, holding himself above me as he stares down into my eyes. I spot some of my cum on the outside of his top lip, dripping into the corner of his mouth.

"You made a mess," he says in a gravelly tone. "Clean it up."

Fuck, I love how bossy he is in these moments. I don't know why. I can't explain it, but he could get me to commit murder if he wanted to.

I place my hands on the sides of his head and bring him down to me, licking the cum from his face before sliding my tongue into his mouth, mimicking his actions the first time we hooked up.

He allows himself to enjoy the kiss for a few seconds before he pulls away and drops down next to me.

Sixteen

DOMINIC

I DON'T SEE Trevor until Monday afternoon when we're in the locker room getting ready to head out to the field.

After we hooked up on Saturday night, we didn't say much to each other. I used the bathroom and put my clothes back on, and when I came out, he was already dressed and in the kitchen. He looked tense, maybe even embarrassed, but I don't know why. He didn't want to look me in my eyes when I came around the corner. It was like he was dismissing me, so I simply said I'd see him around and walked out.

This thing with Trevor is a strange and new experience. I think it's pretty obvious we have chemistry, even if he doesn't want to admit it. His frustrations with me stem from his feelings for me, even if they're just sexual. He fights so hard to keep from giving in, but when he does, it's fucking beautiful. He's the perfect listener—so eager and ready to do anything I say. He wants me to tell him what to do. He needs someone to control the situation, because otherwise he'd be in his head too much. I know he loves it, but once it's over, the mood shifts, and he's back in his head. I've never been with someone who can't admit how much they like what we're doing.

At my locker, I rip off my shirt, kick off my shoes, and start pulling out my football gear. Trevor rounds the corner and halts briefly when he sees me, before realizing he has no choice but to pass me to get to his locker.

From a couple feet away, Jay turns and says, "Hey, did y'all have fun?"

Trevor's eyes narrow at me before I focus on Jay. "This weekend? Yeah. I had a good time."

"I didn't get home 'till five-thirty Sunday morning," Jay says with a laugh.

Trevor's shoulder relax once he realizes Jay wasn't insinuating anything. "Yeah, it was cool."

"I saw you talking to Naomi for a little while," Jay tells him. "Liv told me she's into you."

Trevor's back is to Jay, but I don't miss his eyes sliding in my direction as he pulls his things out of the locker. "Oh?"

"Yeah, you want her number?"

He sighs, scratching the space between his brows. "Nah. I mean, she's cute, but..." He trails off, unsure what to say.

Jay shrugs. "I'll tell Liv you're not interested. She wanted to play matchmaker."

Trevor turns and forces a smile. "I'm good. No need."

"I know you're not a relationship kind of guy," he says with a wink. He pulls his jersey over his shoulder pads and looks at me. "Oh, dude, I met this guy. He's not really my type, but you might like him. I can introduce you."

I don't miss the stiffness re-enter Trevor's shoulders as he tries to avoid gazing in my direction.

I laugh. "He's not your type? What does that mean? He ugly?"

Jay laughs. "No, man. I wouldn't hook you up with an ugly dude. He's attractive, but he's...I don't know. Too innocent. Does that make sense? I don't know," he says again with a shrug. "What's your type?"

"I do like them innocent," I say, leering at Trevor as Jay has his back turned. "I don't mind teaching them a few things."

Trevor quickly finishes up, and Jay laughs.

"See y'all out there," Trevor says as he rushes off.

"What's up with him?" Jay questions.

I shrug, and we change the topic as we head to the field together.

Practice goes well. For me. Trevor has an off day and Coach gets on to him quite a bit. Our first game is Friday and Coach told him he better get his shit together before then or he won't be playing.

On the way back to the locker room, Dex jogs up to Trevor, who's only a few steps ahead of me and asks, "You okay, man?"

"I'm fine!" he snaps at him.

Dex jolts back slightly. "Okay. Just checking."

"Why? Because I had such a shitty day? I guess I'm the only one who has off days."

Dex looks back at Jay who's between me and them, confusion on his face. "No, I didn't say that."

"I'm fine. Just in my head too much. I'll be fine."

"All right, man," Dex says before running ahead.

I decide I need to talk to Trevor, but considering his mood, I already know he's gonna be pissed the minute I approach him.

While I'm in the shower, the loud voices eventually turn into a dull roar, followed by a few quiet goodbyes as people start leaving. I let the hot water hit my shoulders and pour down my back, hoping to relax some of the soreness in my muscles.

I take my time getting dry and dressed, enjoying the rare silence of a locker room. Coach's voice is audible from behind the closed door of his office, but other than that, it's quiet.

A couple minutes later, the door creaks open and a furious looking Trevor storms out of his office, glancing at me briefly before pushing through the main doors.

Several minutes later, when I finally emerge outside with my bag hooked over my shoulder, I'm surprised to see Trevor at a bench halfway between the athletic building and the parking lot. His legs bounce while his eyes are trained at the space between his feet.

I think to stop and ask him if he's okay, but I'm not in the mood to get snapped on, so I stroll by. I've only taken a few steps past him before he gets my attention.

"Hey!"

I stop and angle my head over my shoulder. "What?"

He pushes up, grabbing his bag and striding toward me. "What happened between us. It can't happen again."

With a snort, I keep walking. "Okay, Campbell."

"I'm serious," he says, following me.

"Right, because you sucking my dick on Saturday is why you were so shitty at practice today."

"You're..." he pauses, searching for his next words. "You're a distraction."

"I didn't even talk to you today. I barely looked at you, and yet, I'm distracting you?" I continue walking to my car as he keeps up with me.

"You don't have to talk to me to distract me. I'm thinking about what we did and whether you told anyone, or if anyone's found out, and I'm searching their faces for weird looks or listening for whispered words about us. I'm too..."

"Afraid?" I offer.

"Is that such a bad thing?" he questions.

At my car, I unlock and open the back door, throwing my bag inside. I close it and lean against it, my arms crossed at my chest. "I haven't told anyone, Campbell, and I won't."

He shakes his head. "Doesn't matter. Look, I just can't."

Annoyed, I let out a huff. "You know what I think? I think you'd feel so much better if you just broke free. Be yourself. Tell people you're gay. Tell them *this is me and fuck you if you don't like it*. Then you don't have to constantly be worried about what they may or may not know. I am not the distraction. You are. You're in your head way too much. Just like on Saturday. As soon as we were out of the bed, you became tense and weird. Why?"

He looks away, chewing his bottom lip, but doesn't say anything.

I sigh. "Whatever, man. You say you don't want to be with me again? That's fine. You're not my only option. But when you keep playing like shit, don't blame me."

His gaze finally settles on my face, and I can see the battle behind his eyes. He doesn't know what the hell he wants, but this weird fucking game isn't for me.

"See ya," I say, hopping in the car and driving off.

Seventeen

DOMINIC

WHEN I GET HOME, I find my mom in the small garden in front of our house.

"What're you doing?" I ask as I make my way to the steps. "It's not really the time to plant flowers."

She laughs lightly and raises her head, pushing her hair out of her face with the back of her gloved hand. "Not planting flowers, but I thought I should clear out this area a little. The weeds have taken over, and I don't even know what the hell this plant is supposed to be, so I'm gonna rip it out. Maybe in the spring I'll plant flowers, but since Halloween is next month, I figure we can put some pumpkins and little decorations over here."

"Might as well leave it as is if you're wanting it to be scary," I say with a laugh.

"Oh," she says, waving her hand at me and shaking her head.

"Want me to help you?"

"No," she replies with a smile. "I like this. I like having something to do, but thank you."

I grin. "Okay. I'm gonna get some homework done before I have to go to work."

"All right, baby."

At the door, I glance back and watch her as she goes back to work, pulling weeds and putting them in a plastic bag. I think I hear her hum lightly. Normally, watching someone do yard work isn't anything spectacular, but I'm happy she's out of the house and doing something other than crying. She's starting to live.

When I get inside, the aroma of food hits my nostrils, and as I inspect the kitchen, I find a slow cooker with what looks like Mexican casserole. I smile, glad that Mom seems to be doing so much better.

I get an hour's worth of homework done before I switch gears and make sure to pay all the bills. Mom's running out of money. Fast. The insurance should come through soon, but it won't stretch too far. I have some money saved, and once I start getting paid for working at the bar, I'll be able to use that, but eventually Mom will have to find a job. Even though she seems to be getting better, I don't want to push her too far too fast. And to be honest, I'm not sure what all she's qualified for.

A knock on my door brings me out of my thoughts. "Yeah?"

Mom pushes the door open slightly. "Will you be able to eat a little before going to work?"

"Yeah, of course," I reply.

She steps in and eyes the envelope to the waste department—the only bill I can't pay online. "Bills? Are we behind on anything?"

"No, we're fine," I answer honestly.

We don't have the extras like cable or five million streaming services. I cut off my Netflix account once I moved here and started helping with bills.

"For how long?"

I press my lips into a line. "Not for too long. The insurance will help, but…"

"I was going to use most of the insurance to pay down the mortgage."

"If that's the case, you'll only have enough for a handful of months or so before you're out of money."

She forces a smile, her eyes glistening. "We'll figure it out. Don't stress yourself out too much. At least you're on scholarship, and we don't have to worry about you dropping out."

I just nod along and follow her to the kitchen where she takes a couple bowls out of the cupboard and starts filling them up.

"Your dad always liked this meal," she says, depositing the dishes on the table as I pull out a pitcher of water from the fridge.

I stiffen, hating hearing about him, but also afraid it will thrust her back into despair. I don't say anything, because I have nothing nice to say about the man. I pour water into two glasses and sit across from her at the table.

Before I can thank her for the meal, she says, "Do you remember the time I cooked this, and your father wanted to help but ended up putting the wrong spices in and it turned out awful?" She laughs at the memory.

"I don't remember."

"Oh. Well, maybe you weren't home at the time."

The only times I wasn't home was when my mom knew my dad would be in a terrible mood or anticipated a fight happening and would send me off to the park or to a friend's house.

"What about that time—"

I cut her off. "Mom, I really don't want to reminisce about him."

Her smile drops and I feel like shit, but I can't sit here and try to remember him being some amazing father and husband. He wasn't. I have no good memories of him.

"I'm sorry. I'm just trying to...I don't know...remember the good times."

"There weren't many, Ma," I say with a sigh. "I can't think of one time where he was good to me."

"That's not true. He loved you."

I keep my eyeroll in check, but my frustration grows. "He loved torturing me. He got off on being able to push me around until I got bigger than him. He was a bully with a god complex, and he was only tough if he was beating up on his wife and kid. He didn't love me. He hated me. Especially when I came out. You don't remember the names he called me? You don't remember him telling me I'd go to hell?"

Mom starts to cry, dabbing at her eyes with a napkin.

"I'm sorry, Mom. If you need to remember him in a fictional light in order to grieve and move on, that's fine, but I can't. You don't know a lot of what me and him went through in the years leading to me moving out. I will not be sad that he's gone and I won't pretend he was decent. I'm sorry for you and what you're going through, but that's it."

She nods. "Okay. I understand." After wiping her tears, she looks me in the eye. "I'm sorry for not doing more. I just didn't know what to do."

"It's fine," I say a little tersely before softening my tone. "I know now that there wasn't much you could do, and if you ever did, you'd pay for it."

"I know it's weird to miss him, or be sad he's gone. I know that," she says, dissolving into tears again. "But I don't know another life. I don't know how to survive. He did everything."

"To keep you from doing anything."

She nods, grabbing another napkin for her nose. "I know."

I get up and walk over to hug her. "I love you. I'm sorry for making you cry."

She shakes her head. "I'm sorry for bringing him up when I know how you feel."

We stay in an embrace for a while until she eventually says she's okay, and I go back to my seat. We enjoy the rest of dinner with talk about school, football, the gossip she's gotten from Ms. Anne next door, and her plans for the garden.

Before I head out to work, I get a text from Jay.

> Hey. That guy I was telling you about? He's down to meet you.

I briefly think about Trevor, but remember he said he doesn't want anything to happen between us again. Maybe it is time to meet someone else.

Eighteen

DOMINIC

ON TUESDAY, Jay texts me after my second class and tells me to meet him in the cafeteria. I usually take food to the library and work there while I eat, but I figure it won't hurt to mix it up a little.

The room is massive, with tons of tables everywhere, luckily my phone beeps with a text from Jay, telling me where to go.

I find him and a few others on the opposite end, near a window. "Hey."

"Hey, man. I just realized I've never seen you in here."

"My class gets out at eleven-twenty, and I usually grab something I can take to the library."

He looks at his watch. "So you've had twenty minutes already. When's your next class?"

"I have another twenty minutes."

"Damn, I wish I scheduled my classes farther apart for lunch purposes. I only have fifteen minutes now, because I was fucking around after my last class."

I laugh. "I just use the time to study."

"Well," he says, putting his hand on the other guy's shoulder. "This is Matthew. Matthew, this is Dominic."

"Hey," I say, tilting my head up as my eyes take him in.

"Hey."

He's definitely cute. His face is soft and smooth, and his warm brown hair is wavy and fairly long, curling up around the base of his neck.

"Matthew isn't into football, but I give him a pass because he's into wrestling."

"You wrestle?" I ask Jay.

"Yep."

"Do you?" I ask Matthew.

He grins, his cheeks blushing. "No, but I don't mind watching."

I chuckle. "I see."

"I fucking hate chemistry. Why did I choose this class?"

I spin around and find Trevor dropping a couple books to the table Liv and Naomi are sitting at behind Jay.

Jay laughs. "Told you to choose biology."

Trevor eyes me briefly before noticing Naomi. Deciding I'm the lesser of two evils, he stands between me and Jay.

I turn my attention back to Matthew, who's telling me something about the last wrestling match he went to.

"I know it doesn't sound like it's fun to watch, but it is."

"Guys in skintight suits? Of course it's fun to watch."

He laughs. "So, you're on the football team?"

"Yeah, our first game is this Friday."

He sinks his teeth into his bottom lip briefly before smiling. "Maybe I'll actually check it out. Guys in tight...pants? Are they pants?" he asks.

Me and Jay laugh, but Trevor looks unamused as his eyes bounce between me and Matthew.

"Anyway, it might be fun to watch that, too," Matthew says. "What's your favorite position?"

I chuckle. "I don't switch positions on the field. I'm always a running back. Unless you're asking about my favorite position in other things."

His face blooms red. "Oh. I didn't mean...but yeah. Okay."

Jay's in the middle of a laughing fit, but Trevor eyes me and then Matthew, before giving me a look like, *really? This guy?*

But he doesn't get to be mad or jealous.

Jay checks his watch again. "Shit, I gotta go. Catch y'all later."

"Oh, me too," Matthew says. "I'll see you around?" he asks me.

"Definitely. Jay knows how to get in touch with me. Maybe I'll see you after the game Friday? We can figure out what your favorite position is."

Okay, I admit I said that mainly to piss Trevor off.

Matthew blushes again. "Yeah. Okay," he says with a smile before walking away.

I let my teeth drag across my bottom lip as I watch him leave, then my eyes land on Trevor. "I like 'em sweet like that. Bet he'll come all over my hand in a few seconds, too."

I wink at him and leave him standing there, fuming.

He's still pissed when he sees me in the locker room, but I ignore him, choosing to talk to Jay about Matthew instead.

After practice is over, Coach calls me to the side.

"How you doin' Hernandez?"

"Everything's good, Coach."

"Your mom?"

"Better, I think."

"And you?"

"I'm fine."

"You're making friends easily, I see. The guys seem to like you."

"Mostly," I answer with a grin. "I'm doin' good, Coach."

He pats me on the shoulder as he walks off. "Good."

Inside, as I'm about to step into my shower, Trevor walks past me. "Did Coach tell you you were starting on Friday, or what?"

My brows furrow. "What're you talking about?"

"I'm assuming it'll be you and Deshawn on the field Friday night."

"Assume what you want, Campbell," I say, hanging my towel on the hook.

"You get in here because you're friends with the coach? Does your family have connections? I heard him ask about your mom."

"Why don't you just shut the fuck up about my mom. You don't know what you're talking about."

He jerks back at my anger, but his face settles into a scowl soon after. "You wanted to talk shit about me being rich and having a house, but you have people getting you into better colleges because of a game of whose parents know who."

I turn and face him. "If that was the case, why wouldn't I have come here in the first place? Just stop, Campbell. It's embarrassing at this point."

"Fuck you."

I laugh before stepping out of my underwear and walking into the shower stall. "You wish."

Nineteen

DOMINIC

I DON'T TALK to Trevor the rest of the week. He does his best to ignore me, but I think Jay's starting to become suspicious, because he tries talking to us both, but the tension is obvious. He asked if we got into a fight, but I shrugged and told him I didn't know him well enough to fight with him.

He guessed it might have to do with who will be starting, and I let him believe that. And on Thursday, Coach informed me I'd be starting with Deshawn. Usually, only one running back is in during a play, but sometimes there's two. He may switch us out, but unless one of us gets hurt, Trevor likely won't play in our first game.

On Friday evening, before we hit the field for the game, Jay runs up to me. "Hey, Matthew is in the stands tonight. Who knows where, but he said he was coming. Guess he wants to try out those positions." He laughs, hitting my arm before he puts his helmet on.

"Good. Hopefully I have something to celebrate."

"For real," Jay says before running ahead.

A few seconds later, Trevor passes me up, meaning he was probably within earshot the whole time.

"Campbell," I call out.

He keeps walking, and I don't have it in me to fight with him, so I let him go.

~

I ran my ass off in the game, rushing for one-hundred and fifteen yards, and scoring one touchdown. Deshawn had another TD, and Jayden caught a beautiful pass from Dex in the endzone for the game winner.

The locker room is loud with excited football players, planning on where we're gonna celebrate tonight.

There's two separate sets of plans, some guys choosing to go to a club, while the others are going to Jay's frat house for a party.

Once showered and dressed, I make my way outside and find Matthew standing with a couple other people. He smiles when he sees me, and I return it.

"Congratulations," he says with a bashful smile.

"Thanks. Did you enjoy the game?"

"It wasn't too bad. I had to ask a lot of questions, but I know you won and that you scored a touchdown."

I smile. "Well, good job."

"We're gonna go," one of his friends says with a grin.

I smile at them while Matthew says goodbye. "So, what do you wanna do?" he asks shyly.

"Well, half the team is celebrating at a frat house, and the other half at a club. I figure I should stop by at least one of them, and then we can run off and do...whatever we want."

"Well, I guess you should know I'm only twenty."

"So, frat house it is," I say, draping my arm over his shoulder and walking to my car.

~

Matthew and I actually stopped for some food before heading to the frat house, so once we arrive, the party is in full effect. We start in the kitchen, taking a shot, and then filling our cups with beer before we go and find Jay and Deshawn playing beer pong against Shea and some girl.

After a couple drinks and a game of beer pong, where me and Matthew lose terribly to Dex and Tim, we move over to a pool table where I find Dex's girlfriend, Violet, playing a game against some guy I don't know.

Matthew has his arm around my waist and his head on my shoulder when I recognize Trevor's friend from the burger place walk up. I think his name's Renzo.

"If you're thinking about playing winner, it's gonna be my sister, and she's gonna take all your money."

I laugh. "I'm good, man. This isn't my kind of game."

"Need the balls to be bigger?" he asks with a chuckle.

"Definitely."

"I'm gonna use the bathroom," Matthew whispers into my ear.

"Okay. We can leave soon, if you want."

He bites his lip and nods, a grin growing.

I turn back and watch Violet sink the eight ball before taking a bow.

"Told you," he says.

Violet smacks him in the arm before collecting money from the guy she just beat.

"So, Trevor's been over there in the corner, sending daggers your way."

I turn around and catch him looking at me from about twenty feet away. He attempts to shift his focus somewhere else, but it was too late.

"Your friend is very confused," I tell him.

"He isn't that confused, he's just afraid."

"Yeah, well, he says he's done with me. Hasn't talked to me in a week, and when we do talk, it's mostly just arguing."

"Minus the night at his house," he says, arching his brow with a knowing smirk.

"So he talks about me?"

"Me and Ronan are the only ones he can talk to, and I don't leave him many options. I don't think he needs to keep everything to himself."

"Yeah, well, the Monday after that night, he said he didn't want anything else to happen. He says I'm a distraction, and I'm done trying to figure out his moods."

"Well, for what it's worth, I think he likes you."

I glance back at Trevor and see him talking to some couple. His eyes slide in my direction before he shifts and gives me more of his back.

"It's not worth much if he's too afraid to tell me he's into me. I'm not asking him to come out, but he doesn't even like to admit anything to me, and he's had my dick in his mouth."

His eyebrows shoot up before he grins. "No offense, but you're new. He hasn't told Jay, and he's known him longer. He hasn't told his parents or his other friends. It's not about you, I don't think."

I shake my head. "That's not what I'm saying. I know I'm nobody to him, but he knows I know. We've done things to each other, and I haven't said a word to anyone. If when we're alone, he can't say he's into me or mutter anything even slightly positive, then what's the point? He was a fun distraction at first, but I don't need the drama."

Before he can say anything, his boyfriend shows up at the same time Matthew comes back, finding us leaning against the wall.

"You ready?" I ask Matthew. He smiles and nods. I look back at Renzo and his boyfriend. "Guess I'll see you around."

Renzo lifts his head, but doesn't say anything.

I've only walked a couple feet before Dex pops up in front of me. "Hell of a game, right?" he asks with a grin.

"Yeah, man. Let's hope we can keep it up."

"I hope so. Anyway, I'm having a party at my place tomorrow. Do you work?"

"Yeah, I go in at six."

"Oh, good. It's gonna be a pool party, so it'll start early. You can come over around two and hang out for a little while before you have to leave."

"Yeah, sure."

"I'll text you the address later. See ya."

Before we can leave the house, one of Matthew's friends runs up, completely trashed, and pulls him into a hug.

"Oh my God, Matt! I didn't expect to see you here. I need Trinity to see you. Come on."

Matthew rolls his eyes and mouths a *sorry* to me before getting dragged off. I head back into the kitchen where Jay hands me a shot glass and demands I drink it in order to celebrate our win properly.

"Where's your boy?" he asks, looking around.

"Who?"

"You got more than one?" he asks, an eyebrow raised. "Not that I'm judging. The more the merrier, I think."

I laugh. "Oh, you mean Matthew?"

He nods, a smile on his face. "Yeah, Matthew."

"One of his friends found him and stole him away somewhere. I don't know."

"You talk to Trev?" he asks, switching directions.

"Uh, no."

"Well, he's mad about not being able to play in our opener, but he still has reason to celebrate. He's too busy sulking in corners and becoming a sad drunk rather than being happy our team won."

I shrug. "Yeah, well, I don't know."

Jayden starts setting up a game on one of the tables, and I have no idea what it's called or how it'll be played, but based on the different types of liquor he's pouring into shot glasses, I know it's gonna get people fucked up.

"Oh shit, can you go to my room and grab my phone? Someone's gonna be texting me soon."

"Yeah, which one?"

"Up the stairs, far room on the left. There's a J on the door."

"Cool."

I jog up the steps and find his door easily, but once in his room I have no idea where to look for the phone. It's not on the dresser or TV stand. I search the bed and end up finding it under a South River fleece blanket.

When I turn around, I find Trevor stepping into the doorway.

My plan is just to move past him, but he stops me with a hand on my arm. My eyes dance from where he's touching me to his eyes before he lets go.

"Can we talk?"

"I have to get this phone to Jay."

A guy walks by the door and Trevor snatches the phone from my hand. "Hey, Lucas. Give this to Jay?"

He tosses it and Lucas catches it easily. "Sure."

"Now?" he questions.

I sigh and step back into the room. As I'm plopping onto the corner of the mattress, Trevor closes and locks the door.

I think to make a suggestive joke, but I bite it back. "What's up, Campbell?" I ask with a sigh.

He rubs his hands together in front him, clearly nervous, and for whatever reason, I find it endearing.

"I know I've been kind of a dick lately."

"Mmhmm," I murmur.

He pins his eyes on me for a second before taking a step

closer. "I didn't mean to claim you're only here and starting because your parents know the coach. I know you're good. I was just annoyed at myself. At everything. I don't know."

I open my mouth to reply, but he keeps going, and considering this seems like a rare vulnerable moment for him, I'm not about to interrupt.

"I talked to Renzo a little bit earlier."

"Is that why you're talking to me?"

So much for not interrupting.

He shrugs, putting his hands in his pockets. "Sort of. I didn't want to..." he sighs, meeting my gaze for a fraction of a second before looking away. "I just didn't want..." He stops again, running a hand through his hair before staring at me. "This is hard for me, okay?"

I pull in my bottom lip, chewing on it for a second before I nod. "Okay."

"I like you...I guess." He chances a glance at me and finds me fighting off a grin. "Mostly," he amends, pressing his lips together in a line. "I don't want you to leave with that guy. It's been killing me watching you with him. I don't want to delve too deep into why that is, besides the fact that I guess I like you, and I don't really want what we've started to come to an end yet."

"You told me that it couldn't happen again."

He perches his ass on a small desk to my left. "Yeah, well, I'm stupid. I thought by saying that I'd make the situation easier for myself, but I'm still thinking about you...and things. Maybe you were right. Maybe if I came out and told people, I'd feel less tension and frustration. But I don't have the same confidence you do. Or Jay does, for that matter. Y'all don't care what people think or say, and I do. I don't know why, but I do. I was supposed to tell my parents and chickened out." He takes a breath. "Regardless of all that, I just wanted to tell you that I want—"

"Me," I say, standing up. "You want me."

He watches me approach him and doesn't look away. "Yeah. I want you."

"In secret."

"For now."

"Okay," I say, coming to a stop between his sprawled legs. "What're you gonna do about it?"

"Uh. What do you mean?" he asks.

"You want me, so what're you gonna do about that?"

"Oh." He bites his lip, looking down before I nudge his chin up with my finger. "I'm not used to...you know."

"Initiating sex."

"Right. Well, I've done it before, with girls, but..."

He rubs his thumb over a small patch on his jeans, becoming flustered and nervous as I reach out and grab his hips.

"I think, then, that we're perfect together. I like being in charge and in control, and you comply so easily." I caress his cheek with my knuckles as he looks into my eyes. "You like it, too, don't you?"

His teeth scrape his bottom lip before he nods. "Yeah. It takes the worry out of the situation. Like you said, I'm in my head too much. With you, I feel free."

My heart flutters at his words. It's one thing to turn someone on, but to bring them a sense of freedom is something I've never experienced before.

I run my fingers through his hair, not taking my eyes off of him. "Don't check out this time. Not ever again. You're free while we're doing sexual things, but as soon as we're done, you climb back into your mind and put up a wall. Let me in, Campbell."

He nods and noise outside brings us out of our own little bubble.

"So, what now?" he asks.

"I guess I need to ditch my date," I tell him with a crooked grin.

"Ugh. How are you into that guy?"

I playfully smack him in the stomach with the back of my hand. "Sounds like someone's jealous."

He purses his lips. "He's not that cute."

"Doesn't hold a candle to you, Campbell. Come on, let's get out of here."

"My place?" he asks.

"Better than mine," I tell him. "I'll leave first and say bye to people, then you come out and I'll meet you at the end of the street."

"Okay."

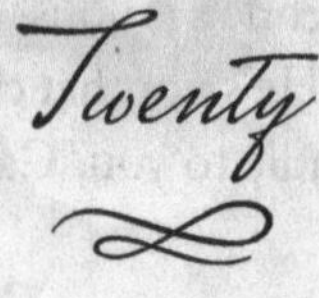

Twenty

DOMINIC

I LIED to Matthew and told him my mom needed me, but he seemed pretty content with his friends and tried to say he'd make it up to me. That won't be necessary, but I'll let him down another day.

After telling Jay I was leaving, I bypassed a group of people and climbed into my car, driving it down the street and around the corner.

It takes ten minutes before Trevor pulls up next to me. I put my window down as he does the same.

"Sober enough to drive?"

He chuckles. "I've definitely sobered up. I'm not too far from here, anyway. Follow me."

"You got it."

Sure enough, it takes less than fifteen minutes to get to his house. When I pull up next to him in the driveway, I poke my head out the window and say, "Hey, did you want me to park somewhere else?"

He shakes his head. "It's fine."

Inside, once the door closes behind us, he tosses his keys to a table and removes his shoes, so I copy him.

"Uhh." He spins around. "Want a drink or something?"

I laugh. "I'm good."

He nervously puts his hands in his pockets, unsure of what to do.

With a smirk on my face, I walk up and grab his hand, tugging him along as I make my way back to his room. "Come on. We have things to do."

Wanting to take my time, I walk him to the side of his queen sized mattress and face him. He's wearing a faded South River football tee, and I slowly lift from the hem until it's over his head and on the floor.

He watches me with a lustful gaze, so I make sure to keep eye contact as I undo the button on his pants, and slowly drag the zipper down. His breathing hikes up a little as I push the denim down his hips until they rest around his knees. He finishes removing them before standing up straight again.

My eyes go directly to his growing erection trying to escape the confines of his navy blue boxer-briefs. I want nothing more than to reach out and stroke him, but I don't. I look him in the eye again and tell him what to do.

"Now you undress me."

He hesitates only briefly before stepping forward and running his hands under my shirt, copping a feel before removing my gray T-shirt and quickly moving to my pants.

Unable to keep my hands to myself any longer, I let my fingers curve around his hip until they rest on his lower back, reaching into the waistband of his boxer-briefs.

I nuzzle my face into his neck, inhaling the citrusy sweet scent of him. "How much have you experimented with?" I ask, my hand dipping lower until I can cup his ass cheek.

His arms wrap around me, his fingers running up the muscles of my back. "You mean...with anal stuff?"

My tongue licks a patch of skin below his earlobe before I murmur, "Mmhmm."

I bring my other hand to his ass, squeezing his cheeks as I grind my cock against his.

He moans, digging his fingers into my skin. "Um. A little."

"We can do a little more tonight, but until you're more comfortable, there won't be any fucking. I don't want to hurt you."

He eases away a little. "What about…"

I arch a questioning brow, my lips twitching. "You fucking me?"

He bites his lip and nods once. "I mean, I've fucked girls before. It's not like I don't know anything."

I let my thumb brush against his bottom lip. "I don't normally bottom. I've only done it a few times."

"Oh."

The look on his face hits me hard. He's new to the dynamics of a gay relationship. He doesn't know what it's like to be fucked by a guy or to fuck a guy. I prefer topping, but honestly, he'd be hard pressed to find something I wouldn't do for him. As long as he enjoys himself. That's what sex is about, right? Satisfying your partner?

"Don't worry about that right now," I tell him, gripping his jaw in my hand. "Kiss me. Kiss me like you want to fuck me, and I just might let you."

He attacks with more confidence than he's ever had. He captures my face between his hands, plunging his tongue into my mouth with a deep moan. I wrap my arms around him, holding him tight against my body as our tongues tangle and twirl before he sucks mine like he's giving it a blowjob.

I push my underwear down, stepping out of them before dropping to the bed, sprawling out for his viewing pleasure. I stroke my length with two languid movements. "Your turn."

He strips, his beautiful cock springing free and pointing at me. "Fuck, you look good," he says.

With a grin and another stroke, I say, "I taste even better."

Without missing a beat, he climbs onto the bed, crawling between my legs and looking up at me with sparkling green eyes. "I do enjoy this part," he says with a small grin.

"Sucking dick?"

"Sucking *your* dick," he clarifies, reaching out to wrap his fingers around me. "I like the way you fuck my mouth."

"Mm." I release a gravelly moan. "You want me to fuck your mouth?"

He looks at my dick, his thumb grazing over the tip and smearing the pre-cum across my crown. When his eyes flicker to mine again, he swipes his lip with his tongue. "I do."

With lightning fast speed, I get up and stand near the bed. "Come here then. Sit on the edge and open wide."

When he does it with eager excitement, I hold his chin between my thumb and forefinger, bending down to kiss him.

"You're fucking perfect."

Straightening up, I cradle his head and slide my cock into his mouth. He hollows his cheeks, sucking me deep, and I begin with slow, long strokes, allowing him to swirl his tongue around my crown before I slide back in.

When I start moving faster and deeper, his cries of pleasure grow. He slurps around my cock, and then his hand goes to his erection, stroking vigorously.

"You love having your mouth fucked, don't you?" I say, knowing he won't answer with words, but a garbled *mmhmm* is good enough for me.

"Move back for me," I say, getting him to lie on his back while I crawl over him.

In the sixty-nine position, I brace myself over him in a way that allows me to move my hips and fuck his mouth while also taking his length into my mouth.

He moans something I can't make out, but I don't stop. I

take him all the way to the edge before I ease away, not ready for him to come yet.

I kneel next to him. "How's your throat?"

He grins with swollen lips. "It's holding up."

"Good. You got lube in here?"

"Yeah. Top drawer," he says, gesturing to his nightstand.

Once I have the lube, I settle between his legs, pour some into my hand and slowly massage some around his entrance while I suck him into my mouth.

He gasps and curses, his hand going to my head.

While I blow him, I gradually slide a fingertip inside his tight hole. I keep my movements slow and gentle, allowing him time to adjust before attempting anything more.

When he starts bearing down on my finger, I ask, "Think you can handle another finger?"

Trevor grips his hair at the root. "Yeah."

With another generous pour of lube, I get two fingers halfway in and pause, giving him time to relax. As a distraction, I wrap my lips around his cock again, stroking it with my free hand before beginning to move my fingers around his ass.

It takes a little while, but eventually, I'm able to thrust two fingers in and out with relative ease, while also taking his dick to the back of my throat.

He's a jumble of noises and hard breaths, his body tensing and squirming while he grips my hair. I curl my fingers up while they're deep in his ass, seeking his prostate.

"Oh shit, oh God, holy fuck," he chants. I keep going, glancing up at him, wanting to see the bliss on his face.

His eyes are squeezed close, his hands moving from his forehead through his hair as his lips part and a sinful breathy moan escapes.

"Yes, that feels so good," he cries. Nothing but moans and hard breathing follow until right before he comes. His mouth opens and his eyes meet mine briefly, and he says, "Dominic."

Then he shatters, his body convulsing as his cum explodes into my mouth. I swallow it down, stroking him past his orgasm, wanting every last drop.

I withdraw my fingers and move up, resting on my knees, enjoying watching his stomach rise and fall with deep breaths. A sheen of sweat glistens over his muscles and he gulps in air like he was just saved from nearly drowning.

"Oh my God," he murmurs, mostly to himself. He opens his eyes and finds me. "Your turn."

My lips pull up on one side before I plant my feet on the floor. "Get on your knees."

His movements are a little slower this time, but he gets on his knees in front of me and grabs the base of my dick before sliding the tip over his tongue.

He takes me deep before withdrawing me from his mouth and flicking his tongue along the underside of my crown.

"Fucking hell," I moan, my hand at the back of his head. "I love watching my cock dip into your mouth." He moans, licking a path down my shaft before making his tongue dance across my balls. "Oh fuck."

He does it a few more times before taking me in his mouth, his hand gently fondling my sac. It's not long before I feel that growing sensation. I hold his head between my hands and fuck into his mouth with steady deep strokes.

"Holy shit, Trevor."

I want to watch my cum hit his tongue, so I step back and stroke myself, holding down his bottom jaw with my free thumb.

Our gazes stay connected until right before my orgasm hits, then I focus on painting his pink tongue white.

"Oh, fuck yes," I moan. "Swallow it down."

He closes his mouth and swallows, his tongue then darting to the corner of his lips, licking up the mess I made on his face. His eyes stay on me, but I see a flicker of something behind them, and I worry he's ready to climb back into his head and shut me out.

I grab him by the throat, pulling him to his feet. "You're so fucking good, you know that?" I press my lips against his, tasting myself on his tongue. I pull away and look him in the eye. "Remember what I said."

He gives me a small grin. "I know. I'm good."

I grope his ass and kiss him again, swiping my tongue across his. "Mm. Yes you are."

"Let's get cleaned up," he says. "Then we can eat, and...I don't know, talk."

I smile. "Okay."

Twenty-One

TREVOR

I TRY to stay out of my head, pushing away intrusive thoughts telling me I shouldn't have done what I just did with Dom—that I shouldn't have given in to my desire. There's a weird sense of embarrassment, like he would judge me, even though I know it makes no sense. And it's not like he's gonna make fun of me for being gay, but for being so eager and willing. Society has ingrained in us that men need to be masculine and dominant, and that only women should be submissive, but I revel in being told what to do in those sexual situations. I think society needs to fuck off and let people be however they want, like whoever they want, and stop trying to fit everyone into tiny little boxes.

I pull out a box of pizza I ordered yesterday and grab a couple plates. "I have some leftover pizza."

"That's cool," he says, watching me from the other side of the island.

"I have some drinks in the fridge. Help yourself."

He saunters over while I place a couple slices on a plate and into the microwave. "You want a Gatorade?" he asks.

"Sure."

119

He tosses a bottle to me and we both twist the caps off, swallowing down a mouthful while watching each other.

"What?" I finally ask after capping the bottle.

Dominic grins. "Nothing."

"Liar."

"Just enjoying watching you try to keep from hiding from me."

I hate that he can see through me. I remove the plate and put it in front of him before warming up my own.

"I'm not hiding."

"Why don't you tell me what you're thinking?"

He picks up a slice, his biceps flexing as he brings it to his mouth. "Um. Nothing really."

"Now who's the liar?" he says while chewing.

I roll my eyes. "It's kind of embarrassing."

He brings his thumb to the corner of his lips, wiping off some sauce. "You don't have anything to be embarrassed about."

I pull my plate from the microwave and stand a couple feet away from him. "Well, you know how earlier we were talking about how I don't really know how to initiate things, and you like to be in control?"

He nods. "Yeah."

"In the moment, when we're intimate, it's easy to forget everything else. Things turn up and you're willing to say and do things that normally you'd never think about doing or saying." His brows draw in as he listens. "I don't know. I like our dynamic, you know, in those moments."

"Okay," he says, dragging the word out, confused.

"But after, I feel like maybe it's weird to be that way. Do you think it's—"

"Weird?" he asks, putting his pizza down. "I know we don't know much about each other, but I'd think you'd know how much I really do like it. You're more submissive in those situations, but that's not a bad thing. I'm more dominant. It's who we are and why we're good together." He grins and winks at me.

I blush and fight off a smile. "Okay, so it's not weird."

"Definitely not."

"You don't look at me differently afterwards?"

"I look at you like I always look at you."

"Which is how?"

He smirks. "Like I like what I see."

"Okay," I reply with a bashful grin.

We eat in silence for a minute before I say, "Can I admit something?"

"Of course."

I don't look him in the eye when I say, "I still want to fuck you, but..."

"But?"

I bring my head up and force myself to look him in the eyes when I say, "But I think I'm more looking forward to how you'll fuck me."

His smile stretches across his face slowly, deviant thoughts shining through his eyes. He rounds the island and stops in front of me, grabbing my hips. "It's gonna be so good, Campbell. You're gonna love the way I fill you up, and I'm gonna love the way you take it." He stares at my mouth briefly before gazing into my eyes. "And as far as you fucking me..."

"I know. You normally top."

He cradles my face, his thumb tracing the edge of my bottom lip. "When it comes to you, nothing that I'm doing is normal."

"What does that mean?" I ask.

He shakes his head. "Doesn't matter. I'd let you fuck me."

"Yeah?" I ask, my breathing becoming heavier as his hand travels down my neck, giving me goosebumps.

"Yeah. And you need to start preparing yourself to take my cock."

"How?"

His arms wrap around me, his hands on my ass through my jeans. "There's toys."

"O-Okay."

He smiles. "I want to watch."

My eyes bulge. "Um."

"Mm," he moans, leaning in and kissing my neck. "I'm getting hard just thinking about it."

"I'm always hard around you," I say, grinding myself against him.

"I like that." He backs up a little, but stays within reach. "You gonna be hard when you see me tomorrow around all your friends?"

"Tomorrow?"

"Dex's pool party."

"Oh, you're going?"

"I'll be there for a little while before I have to go to work."

"Well, shit. Please tell me you're going to the pool party in a hoodie and sweats."

He laughs. "Afraid not."

"Great."

"Do you work?" he asks, changing subjects as he hops onto the counter.

"No. My parents want me to focus on school."

"I'm assuming they give you money then."

"Yeah. They have a good amount of money. Plus my grandparents on my Mom's side died and left me a good amount"

"What do your parents do?"

"Mom's a lawyer in her own firm. Dad's an investment banker."

He nods. "Cool."

"And yours?"

Dominic twists his mouth to the side, chewing on the inside of his bottom lip. "I'm not like your friends, Campbell," he says. "You all seem to be pretty well off with perfect families and perfect lives."

"You can't judge someone from what it looks like on the outside."

He dips his head. "Touché." After a deep breath, he says, "My dad died. That's why I'm here. My mom needed help, and I live with her to make sure she's okay, to keep things afloat, and right now I'm the only one working."

My eyes widen as air rushes from my lungs. "Oh my God. I'm so sorry, Dominic. That's...wow, that's gotta be awful."

He snorts, surprising me. "Dear old Dad isn't missed. Not by me anyway, so don't feel bad about that."

My shock turns to confusion, but based on his tone, there's something way deeper there, and I don't think it's my place to push him to go into details.

We're both quiet for a while, but he breaks the silence. "So, anyway." He hops off the counter. "I'll be sure to wear my speedo for you tomorrow."

I grin, shaking my head. "Please don't."

"I had fun tonight," he says, hands in his pockets as he watches me.

"Me too."

"Give me your number so I can annoy you via text."

I chuckle. "Give me your phone then."

He pulls it from his pocket and hands it over. "I expect a lot of dick pics."

I bark out a laugh. "You send one first."

"Think I won't."

I give him back his phone. "I know you will."

He takes his phone with one hand, grabbing my wrist

with the other and tugging me into him. "Or we can Face-Time while you fuck yourself with a toy."

"Oh God."

"Mm. Yeah, I want to hear you moan those words."

I eye his lips, wanting to kiss him again. He notices but doesn't make a move, instead waiting to see what I do.

I lean forward slightly, and when he still doesn't come forward, I just press my lips against his, grabbing the back of his neck. His hand pushes against my ass, bringing our bodies closer.

When he pulls away, he studies my face for a few seconds before saying, "See you tomorrow."

I nod once. "Yeah. Tomorrow."

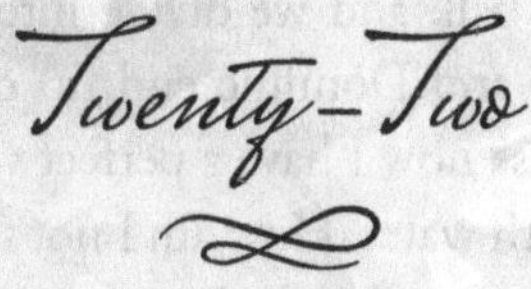

TREVOR

FROM THE WHITE chaise lounge chair at the side of the pool, I watch as Dex carries Vi on his shoulders, playing chicken with Jayden and a girl named Tiffany. On the other side, Ronan, Renzo, Tim, and Deshawn play a game of basketball with the poolside hoops.

Dominic hasn't shown up yet, and my stomach is knotted up with nerves waiting for him to strut back here. Next to me, Shea and his girlfriend, Shannon, are basically dry humping, moaning with every kiss, so I get up and head to the shaded area to grab a drink from the cooler.

As I watch the scene in the pool, the door behind me opens. I glance back, expecting to see Dex's dad, but instead, Dominic's hulking figure emerges.

He grins. "Waiting for me?"

"Maybe."

"This house is crazy," he says, closing the door.

"Dex's dad owns a billion dollar company."

"Yeah, looks like it. Jesus Christ. I've never seen so many nice houses in one place until I drove up here."

"Hey! Hernandez," Tim yells from the pool.

He raises his hand and starts walking over. I take a breath and try to remind myself not to stare at him too closely when he takes off his shirt to get in the pool.

After a few minutes, Dex gets out and grabs the inflatable volleyball net and ball, and we divide into teams and play a couple games. Me and Dominic end up on opposite teams, which sucks because now I have a perfect view of his muscled body glistening with water. How am I not supposed to stare?

When we stop for a break, Dominic climbs out, and his shorts are plastered to his thighs, making a certain part of him very visible. My eyes linger for a second before I meet his gaze. He winks and I turn away, thankful nobody was paying attention.

"I'm starving," Renzo complains.

"I ordered pizza," Dex says. "It'll be here soon."

"Dude, we need to go back to Toast. I want to try that bull again," Tim says.

"Your ass could barely hold on the first time," Shea replies with a laugh.

"Exactly. I'll try it sober this time."

"These two did pretty good," Shea says, pointing at Jay and Dominic.

"We were so fucking drunk," Jay says. "I don't know how we stayed on for as long as we did."

"Which was only a few seconds," Dom adds.

"When do you turn twenty-one, Campbell?" Dominic asks me.

"In a few weeks."

"Let's plan to go then," Dom says, looking at the rest of the guys. "We can get Campbell drunk."

Everyone agrees to go out on my birthday weekend, then we start talking about different topics, the conversations breaking up into groups.

Dominic stands next to me as I sit in one of the chairs and

asks me if I've seen some movie. When I tell him I have, we make fun of the plot, but then he says, "The guy was hot, though." I almost agree, but instead laugh.

Jay's nearby and says, "Well, it looks like you two kissed and made up."

"What?" I question.

He laughs. "Don't even act like you weren't being stand-offish and weird around him."

"I guess I was just in a mood. I don't know. It's not a big deal."

"I'm pretty charming," Dom jokes. "It's hard not to like me."

I shake my head, but refuse to look at him because I may blush.

Dex's dad comes out wearing an expensive looking suit, carrying pizzas. "Dex, I gotta get back to the office. Someone's threatening to quit."

Dex takes the pizzas from his dad. "Who? Why?"

His dad shakes his head. "One of the secretaries, and I don't know why."

"Okay."

He says bye to everyone before rushing off, his phone already to his ear.

The rest of us sit around and devour the pizza. I find it's not too hard to be around Dominic. Yeah, my eyes keep finding their way to him, and yes, I can't stop thinking about how much I want to kiss and touch him, but at least I'm not acting it out. At least nobody's caught me staring when I shouldn't be.

"I hate that I have to go to work," Dom says.

"Yeah, because Dex has an inflatable beer pong table, and when the sun goes down, we're gonna play that in the pool," Tim says.

"Just rub it in my face, asshole," Dominic says with a laugh, standing up and stretching.

It's really hard not to stare at how his muscles flex, but I glance at him briefly before taking a sip of my Coke. Renzo waggles his brows at me, but I ignore him.

"I gotta head out," Jay says. "We're gonna go watch a movie," he says, gesturing to Tiffany. "I might come back later though. I'll text you," he tells Dex.

"Okay, cool. We'll be here."

"I'm gonna grab another drink," I say, crushing the empty can in my hand.

"Can I use your bathroom before I leave?" Dominic asks Dex.

"Yeah, if you go through the door, cross the kitchen, turn right, and then to the left the hall will lead to the bathroom."

Dominic raises his brows before laughing. "Okay, if I'm not back in ten minutes, send a search party."

"Trev, will you show him?" Dex says as I'm heading to the cooler.

"All right," I reply, trying not to show my excitement at a chance alone with him.

Inside, I toss my can into the recycle bin as we're in the kitchen, then make my way to the bathroom.

"See, I told you there's something up with us and bathrooms," he says from behind me.

In the hall, I spin around and push him against the wall, slamming my mouth to his in a desperate kiss.

He's taken by surprise at first, then he grabs a hold of my ass and brings me in closer, massaging my tongue with his.

When we separate, he says, "As much as I enjoy pliable Trevor, I kinda like you like this, too."

I smirk. "I was dying to do that."

"I'm glad you're willing to show me how much you want me now, instead of fighting it."

I roll my eyes. "Go to the bathroom."

"Come with me."

I almost go with him, but decide it's too risky. "I can't. Anybody could come in." He nods his head slightly, like he knew that would be my answer. "But maybe I can go by your job later. Everyone will be here. I can wait for you to get off."

He smiles. "Okay. Now kiss me again."

Twenty-Three

TREVOR

AS TO NOT BE TOO OBVIOUS, I stick around Dex's house for a few hours after Dominic leaves. My excuse was that I needed to study, which isn't a lie, because I need to, but I'd rather study Dominic.

I went home first, to shower and clean up, because I hope he'll come back with me for a little while once he's off. Since I know he lives with his mom, I doubt going there is an option.

By the time I show up to Three Sheets and get my neon bracelet and big black X on my hand, it's ten-forty. I choose a booth with a good view of the bar, and order a burger and fries to go with my Coke. Luckily they have a sports channel on, so I'm not too bored sitting here alone.

It's about twenty minutes after I arrive when Dominic emerges from the back, collecting empty bottles and glasses, and restocking the bar with straws and napkins. I can't help but smile when I watch him move, the tight black shirt clinging to his muscles the way I want to.

He speaks to one of the bartenders for a little bit before disappearing into the back and coming back with a black plastic tub. We finally make eye contact as he heads for a nearby table.

"Stalking me, Campbell?"

"I think stalking is unwanted attention, and I don't think that applies here."

He smirks, clearing the table. "I guess you're right."

"Where do the guys think you went?" he asks, moving the tub full of dishes to a chair so he can wipe it off.

"Studying. Which isn't really a lie."

He snorts. "You're studying me?"

"I want to memorize every part of you," I admit quietly, wondering where this confidence came from.

Dominic's head swivels, an eyebrow arched. "Interesting." He finishes wiping down the table before turning to face me. "Maybe I'll let you do that tonight, just so I can make sure you don't become a liar."

"Too late for that probably," I say, picking up a fry.

"I wouldn't say not coming out is lying. You're not ready. If they're your friends, they'll understand that."

I shrug. "So, you'll come over?" I ask, my tone hopeful.

Dominic's lips turn up on the ends, giving me a joyful smile. "Yeah, I will, but..." He pauses, looking me over. "I want you to do something for me first."

I wipe my mouth with the back of my hand and swallow my food. "Like what?"

"I want you to go to the bathroom and send me a picture of your cock."

My eyebrows shoot up. "Right now?"

He nods, a small smile forming, his eyes daring me to do it. "Before I get off work."

"You want me to get hard enough to take a decent picture, but you don't want me to come?" I whisper.

"Oh, you better not come. That's for me later."

My dick twitches at the thought and I shift. "Um. Okay."

"Good boy," he says, his tongue dancing slowly across his bottom lip as his eyes drink me in.

He leaves before I can say anything else, so I try to get back to focusing on my food. He's in and out of the back, walking around the room, and I can't keep my eyes off of him. Another guy comes by, trying to take my plate, but Dominic approaches from the other side.

"I got it."

The guy nods and heads to the back.

I stare up at him, envisioning all the things I want us to do—everything I want him to tell me to do.

"Whatcha thinkin' about, Campbell?" he asks with a light laugh.

"Just some things."

"Like what?"

I clear my throat. "Just anxious to get back home with you."

"Yeah? Well, I won't be going anywhere until a certain photo hits my phone."

With a glance at my watch, I say, "I have some time."

He smiles at me. "Okay."

When he disappears into the back for a while, I choose that time to go to the bathroom, locking myself in one of the stalls. I turn the volume down on my phone and bring up a porn site, but while I watch two guys going at it, I imagine it's me and Dom. I think about what it would be like to have him slide into my ass. Then I wonder how it would feel to be inside of him. Thoughts of him fucking my mouth flash in my head, and I realize now that my eyes are closed and all I'm thinking about is the times I've had with him. My erection is rock hard in my hand, and I'm nearly close to coming.

"Fuck," I hiss, letting go.

I exit out of the porn and open my camera up. Before taking a picture, I decide to do him one better. I slide it to video and record a short clip of me stroking my dick. Pre-cum glistens at my tip, and I slide my thumb across it before turning the camera to face me while I lick the arousal from my finger.

I send it to him before fixing my pants and buttoning them back up, my dick still painfully hard and tucked behind the waistband of my boxer-briefs.

Leaning against the wall of the stall, I try to think about anything other than him so my dick can start to soften. Less than a minute later, the door to the bathroom opens with a squeak and heavy footsteps march in.

"Trevor." Dominic growls my name.

I unlock and open the door, only for him to force himself inside and push me against the wall. He grabs my face and devours my mouth in a brutal kiss. It doesn't last nearly long enough, but it definitely brings my cock raging back to life.

He pulls away, staring into my eyes as he adjusts himself quickly before turning and leaving. Before the door closes, he says, "I'll be there."

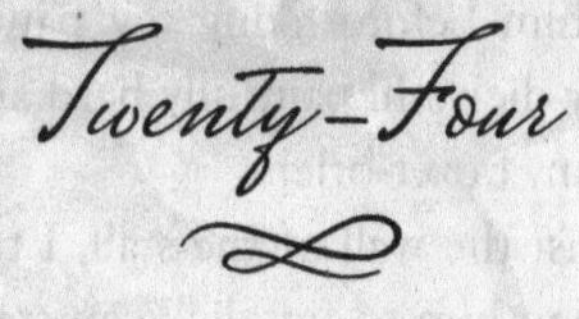

TREVOR

I DECIDE NOT to stick around until closing time. After confirming with Dominic my address so he can get there on his own, I leave Three Sheets and head home.

Around a half an hour before he's set to be here, he texts me.

> I'll be leaving in a little while. Do me another favor?

> What're you gonna do for me?

> You know I'm willing to do any and everything. I'll make you feel good. Don't worry about that.

> What is it?

He doesn't respond right away, probably caught up with work, but I hold my phone, grinning like a fucking idiot at his last message.

I'm assuming you don't have any toys yet, but you can use your fingers. Show me how you're preparing yourself for my cock.

Are we doing that tonight?

Regardless of what we do tonight, you'll need to be ready for me soon.

I don't tell him that he's wrong—that I do have a toy. I actually went out and got one earlier today from the next town over that has a sex toy shop. It's nothing compared to the size of Dominic's dick, but it's something. I've been doing research on what to do and what to expect, so I've already cleaned everything that needs to be cleaned.

Pulling out the smooth, black silicone toy, I make sure to wash it and then grab the lube I bought at the same place. It only goes in about four and a half inches, but looking at the slightly curved shape makes me nervous. It's supposed to be a good prostate massager, but I can't even think about turning on the vibrations yet.

I strip out of my pants and boxer-briefs and lie across the bed, pulling up a porn video on my phone. After a few minutes of stroking myself to a clip of a man who's fucking himself with a dildo, I squirt some lube on my hand and start with penetrating myself with my finger before moving on to the toy.

It's nearly ten minutes before I feel comfortable sliding it in and out at a slow pace, but it doesn't feel bad.

I remember Dominic wanting visual evidence, so I set my phone on my nightstand, propped against the lamp, and spin around to give him a better view.

I've never recorded myself like this. Hell, I've never done this, but of course I'm willing to do it for him. I want nothing more than to be able to take him in my ass, and it's not like he hasn't been acquainted with every part of me already.

Still, I feel nervous as I slide the toy in and out while lying on my back. I angle to the side a little, pushing it in with one hand as I stroke myself with the other. I moan, enjoying the pleasure.

I edit the video to right under a minute and send it to him without any text. While I wait for his reply, I keep fucking myself with the toy, finding I love it more with each passing second.

Five minutes later, my phone lights up with a FaceTime call from Dominic.

"Hey," I greet, holding the phone over my face as I continue to lay on the bed.

"You're trying to kill me, aren't you?" His face is barely visible, shrouded in the dark.

I chuckle. "You asked for it."

"I didn't know you had a toy."

"I got it today," I say.

"Are you still using it?" he asks, his voice getting husky.

I shift, moving the toy. "Maybe."

He groans. "I wanna watch."

"Then hurry up and get here."

"I'm already close."

"Me too," I say teasingly, biting my lip.

"You better not. Is your door locked?"

"No," I say breathily.

"I'll see you soon."

He hangs up and I drop my phone next to me, continuing to tease myself with the toy while I wait. A few minutes later, I hear the front door open and close, and then footsteps head in my direction.

My heart rate spikes, knowing he's getting closer. The lights in my room are dim, the bedroom lamp set on the lowest setting. When he rounds the corner, his eyes flash with desire when he spots me.

"I could get used to this," he says, toeing off his shoes and removing his shirt.

"Good," I basically moan.

Before he gets to the bed, he's stripped of everything except his boxer-briefs. He settles next to my legs, his hand running from my knee, up my thigh, and his eyes trained between my legs.

"Let me," he offers in a low tone, reaching for the toy.

I let go as he grabs hold, my eyes locked on him. When he meets my gaze again, he leans down and gives me a small kiss.

"Does it feel good?" he whispers against my lips.

I nod. "Yeah."

"Looks fucking phenomenal," he says, easing back to watch the toy disappear inside of me. "Stroke yourself."

My hand grabs my cock, slowly jerking it a couple times, before saying, "You should get it wet."

His brows quirk up, a grin on his lips. "Oh, should I?"

I dig my teeth into my bottom lip, smiling at him. "I'd appreciate it."

Dominic changes positions, getting in between my legs and taking my cock in his mouth while still penetrating me with the massager.

"Oh, God."

It feels incredible having both sensations happening at the same time. My cock grows even harder, and when he backs up, releasing me from his mouth, I take hold and stroke, staring him in the eye.

"I wanna fuck you so bad," he growls. "But until you're fully ready, I guess you'll have to fuck me."

My eyes widen. "Tonight?"

"Right now."

"O-okay."

He smirks, getting up to remove his boxer-briefs and then reaching for the lube next to me. "You got a condom here?"

I remove the toy—very cautiously, and get up to grab a condom from my dresser. As I walk back to the bed, his eyes drink me in. He strokes himself a little bit before reaching around and sliding his lubed up fingers between his cheeks.

"Lay down," he commands.

I assumed I'd fuck him while he was bent over, but apparently he has other plans, and at this point, I'm too much of a beggar to be a chooser. I'll take what I can get.

He gets on his knees on the mattress, and I wait for what's gonna happen next. Snatching the condom up, he tears it open and easily rolls it down my shaft before squirting a liberal amount of lube on his hand and coating the latex. Reaching back, he slathers more on himself and then straddles me.

I bite my lip as I watch his huge muscular body settle on top of mine. I love the weight of him, and the roughness of the hair on his legs against mine.

At a torturously slow pace, he guides me into his tight warmth until he's fully seated.

"Fuck," I grunt, my hands running up his thighs until I grab ahold of his hips. "Oh my God."

He moans, slowly rocking back and forth. This viewpoint has got to be the best there is. This sinfully sexy god of a man sits atop me, his muscles flexing and his face contorted with pleasure as he moves.

It doesn't matter that I'm the one penetrating him, because he's clearly still the one fucking me, his movements growing faster and more comfortable. He places one hand behind him, resting on my thigh as the other one presses against my chest, and he rides me like a fucking pro.

"Jesus Christ," I moan, touching his abs and chest. "You feel so good."

"You do," he replies in a breathy tone. "Fuck. Touch me, Campbell," he says, dropping his head back.

I take his cock in my hand, stroking him as he moves.

After a few minutes, I say, "Hold on," and move up, getting into a sitting position as my back rests against the headboard.

He grabs my jaw and presses his mouth to mine, kissing me passionately as I hold him around the waist. I raise and lower my hips, pushing into him gently at first to see if he's okay with it.

When he says, "Yeah. Fuck me." I know he's into it, so I push deeper.

With a hand on my throat, he turns my head and kisses and licks the side of my neck before sucking a patch of skin so hard I'm sure I'll be left with a mark. But I don't care. I want his mark on me just like I want his hands on me. I want his everything.

"Oh my God," he moans into my ear.

"Kiss me."

He does, massaging my tongue with his in a sensual caress. "Give me your tongue," he pants after pulling away.

I stick my tongue out and he closes his lips around it, sucking on it like he's siphoning his favorite drink. That paired with his tight ass clenching around my cock, I know I don't have long before I come.

With a desperate moan, I pull away. "I'm gonna come if you keep it up."

He kisses me. "Kind of the point."

"You come first. I want it all over me."

He groans. "Fuck, Campbell. What're you trying to do to me?"

"Ruin you for anyone else."

Something flashes in his eyes, but I can't tell what it is. He simply says, "Hmm," but it sounds like a moan as he leans back, his cock protruding between us. "Touch me, then. Ruin me."

I take it as a challenge, using one and then both hands on his cock as he keeps his steady motion on my cock. When he's not moving back and forth, he lifts up and down, driving both of us crazy.

I spit on my hands and continue to stroke him, my movements quickening when he speeds up, seeking out that pleasure spot.

My teeth dig into my bottom lip as I watch him. He's fucking perfect. So handsome you wonder how he exists in the same world as you. How is he not in a magazine or on TV?

When his eyes open and connect with mine, we don't look away.

"Come on me," I breathe. "I want to feel it."

His mouth parts as his eyes close and head drops back between his shoulders. "Oh God."

I watch as cum shoots from his cock, landing in ribbons on my stomach and chest. It's so fucking hot it sends a jolt of desire through my veins, making my stomach clench and my balls draw tight.

"Oh shit," I cry out, holding onto his hips as he rocks back and forth. "Fuck. Dom."

My fingers dig into him as my orgasm hits, and I arch off the headboard, my head resting against his shoulder as my body tenses.

We both take several seconds to come down from the high, breathing heavily, our sweat-slicked bodies against one another.

When he moves to get off, I grab the base of my dick, making sure the condom stays on. He flops next to me as I remove and tie off the latex.

"Gonna wash up," he says, rolling over and holding out his hand. "I'll take that."

I drop it in his hand, and when he closes the bathroom door, I take the opportunity to go to the other bathroom to clean up as well.

When I make it back to the bedroom, he's already in my bed, under the covers. He grins. "Too soon for a sleepover?"

I chuckle, an overwhelming sense of excitement growing in my stomach and spreading to my chest. "No, I think it's perfect timing."

I get in bed next to him and he stretches his arm out, patting on his chest, telling me to lay on him. Which I do.

"That was so fucking good," he breathes, his fingers running up and down my tricep.

"Yeah it was."

We lay in silence for a while, and I begin to wonder if he fell asleep, but he finally speaks up.

"I like you, Trevor."

The use of my first name catches me off guard. He doesn't use it often, and it makes my heart stutter in my chest when I hear it, along with the message.

"I like you, too."

He chuckles, and I wonder if it became too serious so he's trying to blow it off. I'm sure he's curious where this could possibly go considering I'm not out. I don't know what to tell him though. I don't want what we're doing to end, but I don't want him to feel like a dirty secret kept in a closet.

"I'm gonna talk to my parents soon," I say quietly.

"Yeah?"

"It's way past due."

"Maybe." He takes a breath. "Don't do it for me."

"What do you mean?"

"Don't come out for me. Make sure you're doing it for yourself."

"I know," I say almost defensively.

"I'm not saying that to be an asshole, but if for some reason we have a falling out, I don't want you to look back at that moment and think you did it for some guy who was just a blip in your life."

I get up on my elbow and look down at him. "A blip?"

He reaches up and caresses my cheek. "Don't get mad. I don't want to be a blip."

I lay back down and we fall silent for several minutes.

"I'm coming out for myself, because I want to be able to talk about you to friends or family. You—a guy I like enough to want to talk about. If we don't end up being anything serious, you'll still be the guy who made me feel something. Who made me not want to hide anymore. That won't change."

He's quiet, and then his arms tighten around me, squeezing me to his side as he kisses my head. "Okay. I can appreciate that."

We fall asleep shortly after, wrapped around each other. Not a worry in the world.

Twenty-Five

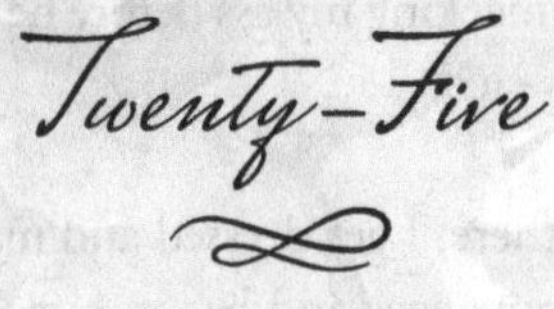

TREVOR

WHEN I WAKE UP, Dominic is knocked out next to me, one arm draped over his head as he lies on his back, and the other hand on my thigh. I grin before I slip away, treading lightly to the bathroom, hoping not to wake him.

After I shower and brush my teeth, I open the door and find him sitting up in bed.

"You should've woke me up," he says with a scratchy voice. "We could've saved water and showered together." His eyes dance over my naked torso, eyeing the towel around my waist.

"Next time."

A brow arches as he stands up, scratching his head. "I think I like the sound of next time." He walks in my direction, groping me through the soft cotton that covers my cock when he stops in front of me. I let out a small moan. "I like the sound of that, too."

"It's not nice to tease."

"Who says?"

I bite my lip, grinning. "Everyone."

"I promise to reward you later," he says, coming in close and nipping at my neck—at the small pink spot he left on me last night. "Since you're such a good boy and all."

I groan. "Fuck. Stop, I'm getting hard already."

He chuckles, smacking my ass before he heads to the bathroom. "Care if I use it?"

"Go ahead."

While he's in there, I get dressed and make my way to the kitchen, pulling some eggs and bacon out. It might be noon, but there's never a bad time for breakfast.

Once everything is nearly done, Dominic struts out wearing the same clothes from yesterday, but smelling exactly like my soap and shampoo.

"I didn't use your toothbrush, but I definitely used your floss and mouthwash."

I chuckle. "Okay."

"Breakfast?" he muses, coming behind me as I stand near the stove, resting his chin on my shoulder.

"Nothing fancy, but food nonetheless."

"I'll take it," he says, grabbing my hips.

His phone rings before I can respond. He steps into the living room as I place the food on the plates.

"Hey. Yeah, I stayed at a friend's house. No. Yeah, I'm fine. You okay? All right. Yeah, I'll be there in a couple hours. Okay. Love you."

After ending the call, he slips the phone back in his pocket and heads toward me. "Sorry. My mom."

"It's cool."

I break off a piece of my toast and pick up a clump of eggs before tossing it in my mouth. He digs in, and while we're silently eating, all I can think about is him saying he stayed at a friend's house. Not that that's not true, though we're slightly more than friends, right? I can't blame him. We're having fun

—secret fun at that, and nobody knows about me, let alone us. If there is an us.

I shake my head as I take another bite.

"You're in your head again," he says from the other side of the table.

"It's nothing."

"You're a terrible liar, Campbell."

I already miss the sound of my first name from his lips. Maybe the fact that he only calls me by my last name is a reflection of how casual this thing is. Last night he said he liked me, but you like your friends, too.

Annoyed with myself, I pull myself out of those thoughts, knowing he'll never think of us as anything serious as long as I'm in the closet and lying to everyone. That's on me, not him.

The doorbell rings incessantly, jolting both of us upright. My eyes widen as my heart beats so hard in my chest it nearly hurts.

Standing up, I creep over to the window and glance to the driveway and see Jayden's car pulled up behind Dominic's.

"Well, shit," I say.

"Who is it?"

"Jay."

He watches me closely, waiting for me to panic. "We can say I just stopped by for something. No big deal. Maybe I needed notes from chemistry class or something."

The bell continues to ring, so I take a breath and walk to the door, pulling it open.

Jay looks confused and somewhat surprised that I even answered. "Hey," he says, dragging the word out slightly. "Umm...is that Dom's car?" he asks, jerking his thumb to what we both know is Dom's car.

"Yeah."

He peeks over my shoulder but can't see where Dominic

sits. "Okay." Again, the word drags out, his eyes studying me and waiting for more.

"Wanna come in?"

I hear Dom's chair slide across the floor and the clattering of dishes like he's hiding evidence of our breakfast together.

"Sure," Jay replies, his eyes landing on my neck.

I back up, allowing him inside before closing the door. My heart is still rapidly beating in my chest, ready to explode. I hope I'm playing it as cool as I think I am.

Dominic's standing in the kitchen, leaning over the island with his phone in his hand. "Hey, man," he greets.

Jay lifts his chin. "Hey. What's goin' on?"

"Not much," Dom says casually. "Just needed some papers from Campbell."

Jay's eyes bounce between us, his eyes once again focusing on the slight hickey on my neck. It's uncomfortably quiet as we all stare at each other.

With a short chuckle, Jay says, "What...is happening?"

I sigh. "Umm." With a quick look at Dominic, I convey as well as I can that I'm about to tell him. Dom dips his head slightly in an acknowledging nod. "Me and Dominic are...kinda messing around."

Dom's lips turn up on one side, amused with how I worded it.

Jay laughs. "I'm sorry, what?" He looks to Dominic for confirmation, but all he does is shrug. "You're kinda messing around? First of all, since when do you like men, and since when with y'all two, because I thought for a minute that y'all were far from friends."

Dominic is no help as he just looks at me, waiting to hear my response, his eyes bright with interest and mirth.

"I've been into guys for a while. I always wondered why I never felt a connection with girls, and while I had a few thoughts here and there, like thinking a guy was attractive, I didn't think it meant anything. I mean, I didn't know for sure until I had this moment with Renzo, and then I decided to pretend that didn't happen and made out with a bunch of girls to convince myself I was straight. When that did nothing for me, I had another, very brief kiss with Zo again, and knew without a doubt that it was men that I was into. When we went to Grand Valley, I uhh...ran into Dominic and we had a moment. Didn't know he'd show up here, so there's that. And yeah, we just kind of re-started things, I guess you could say?" I look to Dom, waiting for him to say something, but he just nods with a smirk on his face.

"I need to sit," Jay says, falling into one of the dining room chairs. "Renzo? Our Renzo? The one with Ronan?"

"It happened before Ronan."

"But that means he knows. Do they both know?"

I nod, putting my hands in my pockets. "Yeah."

"And y'all fuckers kept it from me? Why?"

I sigh. "I don't know, man. Nobody else knows. I don't know how to tell people, and my parents don't even know. It was nothing against you. Renzo only knew because it was him who I, you know, did stuff with. Of course he told his boyfriend."

"Jesus Christ, man," he says. "I...well, I'm shocked, but probably more so that you're with this guy," he says with a good-natured grin, glancing at Dominic.

"Yeah, well, he's pretty persistent."

"He likes it, though," Dom says, finally speaking up.

Jay laughs again, his hands going to his face. "I can't deal with y'all. This shit's crazy. So, what is this? Just casual hooking up? Experimenting on your part?" he questions, looking at me.

Me and Dom turn to each other, neither one of us answering. I finally say, "I don't know."

Jay chuckles again, shaking his head. "Well, I'm happy for you. I'm glad you're taking steps to be your authentic self."

"A few more steps to go, I guess."

"You'll get there," he says. "Now, let's talk about our game at Glen Prep, and then plan your birthday party."

I grin, happy that my coming out moment to Jay wasn't nearly as traumatic as I imagined it would be. But if I'm being honest, I never thought he'd react negatively. It's other people I'm more concerned with.

As I sit in the driveway of my parents' house, I think about all the ways this can go wrong. I didn't tell anyone I was coming to talk to them, just in case I chicken out. Once Jayden left, Dominic only hung around for a few more minutes before he left for his house, and I decided to drive out here and get it over with.

But now my fear is getting the better of me. My parents and I have a decent relationship. We don't talk every single day, but I usually check in every week or so. We live half an hour away from each other, so it's not too far, and I definitely visit for major holidays. They've been to a handful of my games, but they aren't too big on football.

I try to flip through a rolodex of memories, attempting to remember if I ever heard either one of them voice an opinion on gay people, gay marriage, or anything like that, and nothing comes to mind. But just because people don't vocalize their hatred for a particular group of people doesn't mean they don't hold those feelings deep inside. I could unlock it right now, and that worries me. I love my parents, and they've always supported me, but would this be the one thing they couldn't get on board with?

My time in my head comes to an end when my mom pulls

open the front door, squinting out at the driveway with her hand over her eyes.

"Trevor? What're you doing out there?"

I take a deep breath and blow it out before stepping outside. "Hey, Mom."

She gathers me in her arms when I get to the porch before holding me at arm's length, looking me over. "What's wrong? You okay?"

I give her a crooked grin. "I'm fine. I can't come visit?"

"Well, you usually call first."

"Is Dad here?"

She opens the screen door and steps inside. "He's down in the basement."

"New project?"

"He's making a little coffee table for me, but with a little cubby in the center, so the top kind of slides out. It'll be cute."

Dad's never been able to say no to Mom and the little things she wants built, but he also enjoys the time down there. He says it's a destresser from his job, so I guess it works out well for both of them.

"You want something to drink, baby?" Mom asks.

"I'm okay. Thanks."

"You still coming down for Thanksgiving?"

"Of course," I reply with a smile. "Think I'm missing out on your food? No, ma'am. I'll be here."

She grins, shaking her head at me. My smile drops when it hits me. Maybe I'll be here. Depends on how they take this news.

"How's school?"

"It's pretty good. Not failing yet."

With a laugh, she says, "Well, that's good. And football?"

"It's good. I guess. I don't know. I had some rough practices and Coach is making me work for my spot, but you know." I shrug. "I'll be fine."

She walks to the doorway that leads to the basement. "Marshall, Trevor's here," she yells down.

I move some pillows out of the way and sit on the gray couch, watching her take a seat on the one opposite me. She watches me with a curious gaze, like she knows something's up. I look away, acting like I'm taking in the room.

"You redecorated."

"A little. You know me and your dad work a lot, so any projects we try to do usually take quite a while. We just finished painting last week, and got some new furniture pieces."

Silence settles over us again as my eyes move between all the photos on the walls and shelves.

"Trevor," she says softly, waiting for me to look at her. I turn my head slowly, my eyes lifting to meet hers. She cocks her head, her brows dipping in the middle. "What—"

"Hey! Look who's here," Dad says, emerging from the basement.

I stand up and give him a hug. "Hey, Dad."

"How are you?" he asks, moving to sit next to Mom.

"I'm good. Mom said you're working on a new project," I say, quickly shifting the focus on him.

"Oh yeah, a new table. I'm about halfway done."

I nod, wondering how to segue into *I'm gay.*

I don't miss when Mom places a hand on Dad's knee, both of them watching me. I sit up and rub my sweaty palms on my jeans. "Um, I wanted to come by and see you guys, you know? And maybe just, I don't know. Talk."

"Okay, well, you know we—" Dad starts.

"Marshall, wait," Mom says, cutting him off.

I study both their faces for several seconds, and emotion

burns at the backs of my eyes as I wonder if this will be the last time I see them happy. Will they kick me out of my house since they own it? Will I lose my parents and a place to live at once? I want to say I know that's not the case, but you can never be too sure.

I lick my lips and take a deep breath. "Um. I—I like. I'm...gay." I let it settle for just a second before I force myself to stare into their eyes. "I'm gay."

They don't say anything right away, but Mom's lips press into a line as her eyes water. "Oh, honey."

The nerves are tied up into a knot in my stomach, and my heart pounds heavily in my chest. I feel like I'm gonna throw up and have a heart attack at once.

Mom rushes over first, sitting next to me and taking my clammy hand in hers. She looks in my eyes and brushes a fallen lock of hair off my forehead. "I'm glad you told us."

Dad stands up and sits on the other side of me, his hand on my back, but he doesn't say anything. I feel this weird sense of relief and confusion.

"You're okay with it?" I question, a lump lodged in my throat.

Mom makes eye contact with Dad before she looks at me again. "Trevor, I thought you might've been years ago."

My eyes widen. "What? How? Why?"

"I thought you and Lorenzo had a thing," she says simply with a shrug. "He was always open about his sexuality and you two spent a lot of time together. I don't know," she says with a shrug.

"Because he was gay you thought I was gay? I also spent time with Dex."

"I know, but you didn't look at Dex the way you looked at Lorenzo."

I shoot up from the couch. "I'm sorry, what?" I laugh with no humor. "I looked at him differently?"

She glances at Dad like she's worried she said too much. "I thought so. Did you not like him?"

I run my hands through my hair. "I—not like that...I don't think. I mean, he's attractive but..." I trail off and start wondering if I always had a crush on my friend and didn't realize it. Is that possible? I was just in awe of him. He had one of those personalities that puts you in a better mood. He was funny and outgoing and I liked being around him.

I shake my head. "Okay, I'm just freaking out a little, but that's besides the point. You thought I was gay and didn't say anything? Why?"

"Me and your father talked about it briefly, but it didn't feel right to bring that to you. I didn't want you to be uncomfortable. I assumed you'd tell me if you were. You just never brought girls over. You went to school dances with your friends and never made mention of dates."

"I've dated girls." Her brows shoot up. "Well, not date." Dad coughs. "Anyway, so, you both thought it was a possibility?"

They both nod, but Dad finally speaks up. "We don't care either way. Like girls, like guys, date both." He shrugs. "As long as you're happy."

I drop down to the empty couch and a sob escapes my throat. The relief I feel is immeasurable. They don't care. They never did. I could've been free sooner, but at this moment, I've never felt happier and more relieved.

They join me on the couch and wrap their arms around me, Mom sobbing next to me as Dad pats and rubs my shoulders.

"I'm sorry for keeping it from you guys for so long," I say, sniffling. "I feel like I've been questioning myself for years, but I went along with what was expected. I don't think I fully accepted the truth until recently."

"Hey, you're our son," Dad says, piercing me with the

green eyes he gave to me. "Nothing could ever change the way we feel about you. We're so proud of you, and we love you more than anything in the world."

The unconditional love they have hits me hard in the chest, causing more tears to leak from my eyes. It's several minutes before I pull myself together. When I do, I decide to tell them one more thing.

"I met someone."

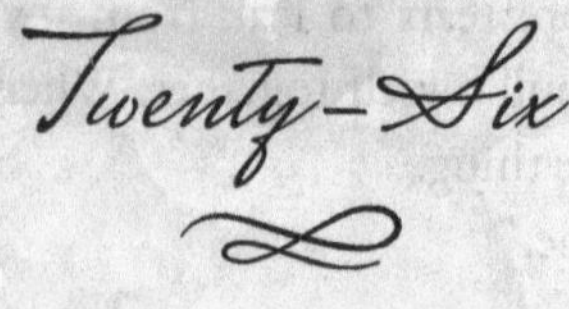

Twenty-Six

DOMINIC

WATCHING Trevor come out to Jayden was pretty endearing. He handled it well, and though I could tell he was looking to me for some help, that was his moment. I don't have any expectations as far as him coming out to everyone now, but at least he felt comfortable enough to tell one of his closest friends.

When I get home, Mom eyes me with amusement from the couch. "Have fun?"

I grin. "Yeah."

"Anyone special?"

I shrug as I sit next to her. "You never know, do you?"

She shifts, placing her mug next to her on the end table. "What do you mean?"

"How do you know if someone is special? You're only seeing what they want you to see in the beginning. Sometimes that lasts a while, but true colors always come out."

"Are you being yourself with him?" she questions.

"Yeah."

"So why do you assume he's putting on a front?"

I look away, staring at the coffee table. I remember me and Mom going to buy this one after my dad pushed me so hard that I fell into the last one and broke it.

"Dad put on a front for a while, didn't he?"

She releases a soft sigh. "I suppose so, but not everyone is your father. I know he disappointed you, and I know he was the only male figure in your life, but not all men will be that way."

When I don't say anything, she continues.

"You've never brought anyone home."

"You know how Dad felt about me being gay."

"You never told me you were dating anyone."

"I've never dated anyone."

"Dominic," she says, putting her hand on my arm and tugging until I look at her. "Why are you closing yourself off?"

I inhale deeply, my shoulders dropping as I blow it out. "If I'm in control, I can make sure things go the way I want them to. If I date someone, it opens up the door to losing that control."

"So you're trying to control your own feelings by keeping things casual?"

"I don't want to become vulnerable, and he's—" I stop myself.

"He who?" she questions.

"This guy I'm...messing around with. I don't know."

"He's making you feel vulnerable?"

"He has the ability to."

"Dominic," she says, joy in her voice. "You really like him. I'm sure he feels the same way about you."

I snort, a grin on my lips. "It's a little complicated. He's not out yet. Not to everyone. And that's fine with me, or it was." I shake my head, trying to get my thoughts together. "Him being closeted was fine when this was just for fun and casual, but now I don't know what's happening, and a few people know about us, and it's starting to feel a little more serious."

"And you're panicking?"

"Internally, maybe. We haven't talked about what we're doing or when it'll end. We're just drawn to each other."

"So he doesn't know where you stand when it comes to relationships?" I shake my head. "Then maybe you need to talk to him."

Feeling uncomfortable with the heaviness of the topic, I switch it. "Maybe. So tell me what you've been up to."

She stares at me for a few seconds, her lips pursed. "Well, I've cleared out some of your father's things—donated half, trashed some others. I redid the room a little to have it a little more to my liking, and I'm going to head out later to do some grocery shopping."

Her bright eyes and smile lets me know she's proud of herself.

"That's good, Mom. I'm happy for you."

"Thank you, honey. I think I'm gonna be okay, you know? I won't lie, I still struggle a little, and part of me wonders if it's because I never got the chance to really tell him how I felt. I had so many fantasies about being brave enough to stand up to him and tell him off before walking out the door, and I never got that moment. Then I feel bad for feeling sad for myself— not because he's dead, but because I didn't get what I wanted."

I take her hand and squeeze. "It's okay to feel like that."

"I never wished him dead," she says. "I'd never wish that on anyone. I just wanted him gone. I hoped he'd get tired of me and just choose to leave."

"He let it be known you'd never be able to leave him," I say. "What happened to him was your way out. If he never died, you'd never be free."

She nods. "Anyway, I'll be okay. We'll be okay."

It's hours later when my phone dings with an alert. I scoot back from the desk in my room where I was doing homework and check it.

Hey

I grin at Trev's simple message.

Hey

He's probably rolling his eyes at me now, because I didn't say more, but I know he has to have texted me for a reason, so this is just me making him get to the point without me having to drag it out of him.

What're you doing right now?

Homework. You?

I just left my parents' house

Oh?

. . .

My heart picks up speed a little and I don't know whether it's out of fear or excitement. Did he come out to them? If so, what does that mean? I like him. I really do. But am I ready for an actual relationship? Does he think that once he's out to everyone that we'll be together? Do I want that? My initial response is *fuck yes*, but my lifetime of trauma comes rearing its ugly head and I think maybe it's best if we keep things casual.

Yeah. You alone? Can I go over?

I've never been too prideful, but after seeing both Trevor and Dex's houses, and knowing all of them come from money, the idea of him seeing my house gives me pause. I'm not a rich kid, and my past is far from ideal. Letting him come over feels a lot like letting him closer to the vulnerable parts of me, and I don't think I'm ready for that.

I can meet you somewhere. That burger place again?

Okay. Be there in fifteen.

It takes me a little over twenty minutes because my house is on the outskirts of town, but when I show up, Trevor's sitting at a table outside, his leg bouncing. When he spots me, it stops, and he grins.

"Hey."

My lips pull up on one end. "You're a man of many words."

He makes a noise, his eyes rolling upwards. "Didn't know there was a specific way I was supposed to greet you."

"The way you greeted me last night is acceptable."

His cheeks flush. "I don't think all these people would appreciate that scene."

I bite down on my lip. "Not like I did."

His smile widens as he glances away, a small chuckle leaving his lips. "Anyway, I wanted to tell you something."

"Okay."

Before he can say anything, Coach Bennett walks by, spotting us. "Oh hey, boys."

"Hey Coach."

"Hey," we both say at the same time.

"Ready for Glen Prep?" he asks.

"I don't know. Will I be playing?" Trevor asks, a little bite in his tone.

"Now you know it's all dependent on your performance at practice. You're good, Campbell. Just distracted, I think."

He looks at me briefly. "Right. Well, I think I'll be good."

"And I'm always good," I say with a wink.

Coach shakes his head, and then does a double take as he gazes behind me. "Camila?"

I jolt around at the sound of my mom's name and sure enough she's strutting this way with a bag in her hand.

"Liam," she says with a small smile. "How nice to see you." Her eyes find me. "Hey, Dom. Who's this?" Her eyes bounce to Trevor who wears a look of confusion.

"This is Trevor."

She looks at me before giving Trevor her attention. "Hi, Trevor."

He smiles. "Hi."

"So, how are you?" Coach asks her, his head doing the sympathetic tilt.

"I'm doing okay," she answers with a nod. "Day by day, you know?"

He nods, crossing his arms over his chest. "That's good to hear. You know you can let me know if you ever need anything."

"I appreciate that," she replies with a grin. "I'm just thankful you helped my boy here."

"Of course," he says. "Well, I guess I'll get out of your hair. See you boys tomorrow."

Once he's gone, Mom lingers. "So..." her eyes bounce between me and Trevor and I know she's wondering if this is the guy I was talking about. "I was just heading down the street to the bakery, then I'm heading home."

"Okay, I won't be out too late. I have more homework to do."

She smiles at Trevor again. "Nice meeting you."

"You too," he replies.

After she's gone, he stares at me with furrowed brows. "So your family does know Coach? And he did help you get on the team? Is that why you're in my spot?"

I sigh, not wanting to fight about this. "It's not like that."

"That's funny, because I literally just heard the conversation. They seem to have a pretty decent relationship, and he helped you. How else did he help you if not by making sure you played on his team?"

"Don't make this into something it's not."

"Then fucking tell me what it is."

"Yes, he helped. So did my coach back at Grand Valley. I told you my dad died. They helped get me transferred."

His anger is palpable. "I think it's much more than that. You didn't even start at Grand Valley, and now you get here where the coach has some sort of relationship with your mom, and now you're starting. You didn't even try out."

I inhale deeply through my nose, trying not to get upset. I can understand how it may look, but I don't like the insinuation of my mom and Coach being in any sort of relationship. "There was no guarantee I'd be a starter, they just wanted to make sure I stayed on the team. My other coach felt like I needed it. The discipline. The distraction."

His eyes narrow on me briefly before he looks away. "Sure."

I sigh, standing up. "Okay, well, believe what you want, Campbell. I'm only starting because I'm better than you."

He shakes his head. "Just perfect."

"What?"

He gazes up at me. "I came out to my parents, and I was so excited to tell you about it, just to have this happen."

"Nothing happened, Campbell."

"Except me finding out why I really got benched."

"You're being ridiculous."

"And you're a lying asshole. I told my parents I had met someone." He laughs humorlessly. "Joke's on me, I guess."

"I didn't tell you to tell them about me. In fact, I told you not to come out because of me."

"I didn't come out for you. I explained that," he says, standing up and meeting my gaze. "And I wanted to tell them about you. I thought—"

"Thought what?"

"Just forget it," he says before turning and storming off.

I watch him leave, hating myself for being such a dick, but he jumped to a conclusion that holds no merit. I'm not starting because of some deal between Coach and my mom.

I should've congratulated him for coming out. I should've

been happy for him, but instead I was angry and frustrated, and the fear of being vulnerable crept back in.

He clearly thought enough about me to tell his parents, and it creates a heady mix of feelings. Happiness, fear, worry, insecurity, and pure bliss.

Twenty-Seven

DOMINIC

MONDAY AND TUESDAY GO BY, and me and Trevor avoid each other like the plague. Jayden is curious considering the last time he saw us we were announcing to him that we'd been hooking up, but he seemed to catch on right away that neither of us wanted to talk about it.

On Wednesday and Thursday, I'm out sick with some sort of stomach bug, which means when I show up to school on Friday, Coach has put Trevor in the starting spot. I'm not even mad. I don't blame him, but Trevor seems to take his place on this team a little more seriously than me.

When we're on the plane, heading for Glen Prep, me and Trevor end up toward the back on opposite sides, with him just a row behind me.

Don't do me any favors. I want to earn my spot. Not have it given to me because you choose to not show up to practice in the days leading up to the game.

. . .

I turn and look at him, but he quickly snaps his attention back to his phone.

> Yeah, I'll be sure to tell my stomach to keep your feelings in mind when I'm throwing up. I didn't just not show up to practice. I wasn't in school at all. Not everything's about you.

He doesn't respond, so I switch the app to Spotify and change the song to blast something loud in my ears while I close my eyes and ignore his presence.

My nap comes to an end a couple hours later—maybe forty minutes before we're due to land, so I get up and head to the bathroom at the back. Trevor's eyes track me as I move, perhaps hoping I'm not coming back to talk to him, but I swear I see a tiny glimmer of hope in those green orbs, but I ignore him and close myself in the small restroom.

I don't know what to do regarding me and him. He's angry at me for something that isn't true, and I'm angry at him for not believing me. I can't keep repeating the same thing, and he's not gonna believe me no matter what anyway. Stubborn ass. On top of that, I worry what squashing the beef between us would mean. Would that put us on the road to a relationship?

When I exit the bathroom and head back to my seat, Trevor's standing up, grabbing his bag from overhead storage and effectively blocking my way.

He glances my way, looking me up and down before

taking his time unzipping the bag and shoving his snacks and bottle of water back inside.

I sigh and he looks at me again. "Need something?"

I force a smile. "Nope."

Once he zips the main pocket, he casually spins it around and unzips another part, just trying to piss me off. Instead of going off on him and drawing attention to us, I grab ahold of his hips as I slowly squeeze past him, pushing my crotch into his ass as I slide past.

"'Scuse me."

He shoots me a dirty look, but I chuckle lightly as I get back into my seat.

Before I know it, we're landing and deplaning.

Jayden comes up next to me. "What's up with you and Trev?"

I shake my head. "He's a stubborn asshole."

"What's his problem?"

"He thinks Coach is playing favorites and only started me the first game because he knows my mom."

"Coach knows your mom?"

I sigh. "It's a whole thing. He knew my parents, but it's not like they were close friends. My dad died and I had to transfer, and both him and my previous coach helped get me transferred. Coach Bennett came to watch me at Grand Valley. That was my tryout, but Campbell thinks it's some sneaky connection thing. I don't even care if I'm a starter or not."

"Sorry about your dad," he says softly.

"Don't be. Anyway, yeah, that's about it."

"But you're not starting this game."

"He thinks I didn't show up to practice on purpose so he could play."

Jayden shakes his head. "Yeah, stubborn. Want me to talk to him?"

"Nah. It's fine. We probably were never gonna be anything serious anyway."

He nods once and the subject is changed.

~

Hours later, after our team won by twenty-four points, we all get settled into our hotel rooms with strict instructions from the coach not to stay out too late, drink too much, or get into any trouble because we're back on the plane early in the morning.

Some will listen, some won't. I already overheard a few guys talking about heading to a club a couple blocks away. Jay asked if I was going out, but I told him no, so I assume he is.

In my room, I drop to the bed and call my mom to check in with her. After a quick conversation, my stomach growls, so I Google a nearby pizza place and decide to order from there. Twenty-five minutes later, I'm in the lobby paying the delivery guy and taking my extra large pizza box.

Passing by the front desk, I hear the clerk say, "I'm sorry. All the restaurants are closed right now. Room service is available but it's a limited menu."

My eyes find Trevor on the other side as he thanks her and turns around to find me. His eyes travel to the box in my hands and then back to my face.

"If you can get over yourself, I'm in room 328. I have more than enough to share."

"I can order my own," he grumbles.

"They close in ten minutes."

I keep walking until I hit the elevators, but he doesn't join me. I'm in my room for twenty minutes, and half the pizza is gone before I hear a knock at the door.

When I pull it open, Trevor wears a look of annoyance already. I'm assuming at himself for actually showing up.

"Hey there."

"I'm only here because I don't want a fruit bowl, pickles, or a sad ham sandwich from room service."

I snort. "Right. Okay." I let him walk past me before I close the door. "Because there are no other food places open in Pennsylvania."

He spins around. "You want me to go?"

"No, I don't. There's a microwave if you want to heat some up."

I sit on the bed, my back against the headboard as my legs stretch almost to the end of the mattress while I flip through the channels. Trevor takes a slice from the box next to me and awkwardly stands near the bed, facing the TV.

"Just sit on the bed, Campbell. I won't bite."

He mutters something before sitting on the edge. I let him scarf down two slices before I speak up again.

"You ready to talk?"

"About what?"

"You tryin' to act like we have nothing to talk about?"

He sighs. "Fine. But you go first."

Twenty-Eight

DOMINIC

"THERE'S nothing I can say that I haven't already. I told you the truth. Yes, my parents know Coach Bennett. They go back several years, but they weren't all buddy-buddy. I hardly knew him at all. I was a kid and I didn't give a fuck who my parents were friends with." I sigh, scratching my jaw. "My dad was an abusive asshole, okay? Coach eventually found out and when he tried to interfere, Dad severed the friendship and Mom wasn't allowed to speak to him again. That's all I know about that, and I only found that out recently."

His face softens and I don't want him to pity me, so I quickly continue. "Don't feel bad for me, Campbell. He's dead and gone now. I'm just sad it didn't come faster. Look, when he died and I started looking into transferring, my coach at GV contacted Bennett and he recognized the name. Because he was fairly aware of our situation, he made sure to help on his end, wanting the transition to move faster and smoother, considering my mom needed me. I would've been able to transfer anyway. He just came down to watch me and that was my try out for the team. Sure, it was special circumstances, but I'm good, and you can't deny that. He knows that, too. I got on the team but you can't say I don't deserve to be on it."

He nods. "Okay."

"And there was no, *my son needs to be a starter* bullshit. My mom doesn't care about football like that. I hardly do. I got into football at GV because I needed it. I was an angry teenager. I was destructive and lashing out and held onto a lot of anger and hurt from my childhood. I needed the discipline that comes with college football. I can't go out and fuck around on the weekends because of games. I don't have free time after school to get in trouble, because I have practice. I don't drink very often, and I workout and take my frustration out on the weights." I shrug. "I have to keep my grades up because of my scholarship, so..."

"You're on a football scholarship?" he asks.

I shake my head. "Academic."

His brows shoot up. "Oh, so you're smart."

"Brilliant," I say with a smile.

He snorts. "Anyway."

"You believe me now, or what? I don't care about that starting spot."

He looks down at the comforter, playing with a loose string. "I'm sorry I was an ass."

"Well, you're lucky I like your ass and am willing to forgive you." His lips purse as he tries to fight off a smile. "I want to apologize too." He gives me a confused look. "You coming out to your parents is a huge deal, and I didn't react the way I should have. I'm happy for you. Really. I'm guessing it went well?"

His lips kick up on the sides. "Yeah. Um, apparently my mom thought I might've been gay years ago."

I laugh. "Moms."

Trevor scoots closer, loosening up. "She might've unlocked some shit I didn't even see back then, but it's fine. They both know and they don't care."

"Good," I say with a grin. "My mom was always okay with my sexuality. My dad wasn't."

He chews on his lip like he isn't sure if he should ask any questions. "Was that why he…"

"Hit me? No. Not the only reason. It started before I was out. It started with my mom. He had addiction issues, anger issues, and who knows what else. Mom doesn't know some of the stuff he said to me when she wasn't around. He called me all the slurs you can think of. Said he'd beat the gay out of me, threatened to force me to sleep with women until I liked it."

My anger builds, my skin prickling with burning rage. Trevor sits right next to me, his leg pressed against mine, and then he takes my hand in his. It's a simple gesture, but it almost breaks me.

"I'm sorry. You didn't deserve any of that."

I bite down on my lip, fearing if I try to speak right now, emotion will get the best of me. I'm mad for being sad about it. I don't like feeling like this.

I shake my head. "Nobody does."

"I feel like shit for being so afraid to tell my parents when that's how your dad reacted."

"I'm just glad you had a better reaction."

"Dominic," he says quietly. I don't look at him. I can't. I'm on the verge of too many emotions. "It's okay to be sad about it."

I shake my head, looking away. "Don't."

I've never allowed myself to be sad. I've only been angry. He squeezes my hand, and a good thirty seconds go by before I feel him move and climb into my lap, straddling me while wrapping his arms around my neck.

I break down, my head on his shoulder as I finally cry about my fucked up childhood.

"I don't know why he always hated me," I sob. "I'm mad my mom never stopped him, but I feel guilty for not being able to save her from him either." He squeezes harder and I wrap my arms around him. "I don't know what I did to deserve that life. I hate him. I hate him. I hate him."

It takes a few minutes before I calm down and pull away, pressing my forehead to his. We stay connected like that for a little bit.

"Thank you," I say. "Sorry for being a mess."

He lifts my face and stares into my eyes. "Don't apologize."

"You've made me vulnerable, Campbell."

"That's okay."

I wipe my face and he eases back but still stays on top of me. "I've never been in a relationship."

"Never?"

"No. I don't like to open up to people. Big surprise, right?" I choke out a laugh. "I don't like being vulnerable. I like controlling the situation, and dating doesn't offer me the same amount of control."

"So, you just do hookups?"

"Basically. There's two people I've been with more than once, and that was twice and three times. Never more than that."

I see the wheels turning. "So, this is temporary?"

"I thought it was. You were in the closet. I didn't have to worry about a relationship."

"But I've started coming out."

"Right."

"So, what now?"

"Exactly. What now?"

We stare at each other for several seconds before he climbs

off my lap and sits next to me. I shift around to face him, because we definitely need to see this conversation to the end.

"What're you thinking?" I ask.

He shakes his head slightly, a couple locks of his blond hair falling across his forehead before he sweeps them back. "I don't know. I uh...I guess I never thought I'd be out of the closet, so I didn't think past secretive hookups."

I nod once. "And now that your parents know, and a few of your friends?"

"I want to be able to be me. I hate living like this—pretending I'm into girls I'm not interested in, lying about why I never have serious relationships, and not being able to talk about...people I like."

I arch a brow. "People?"

He grins, but doesn't clarify. "But what about you? I think we've surpassed being together three times."

"We've only had sex once, and I've yet to sink into that ass, so..."

"So, you don't count blowjobs and handjobs?"

I chuckle. "I don't know what the hell I'm doing, Campbell."

"What if I never sleep with you? Then technically we'll never surpass your three time limit."

My smile widens. "So, you don't want this to stop? This thing between us?"

He looks confused. "Of course not."

"I'm the second guy you've been with. I don't know what the hell you and Renzo did, and please spare me the details, but don't you want to go out and explore? See what you like?"

He turns his head, staring down at his jeans. He's quiet for a little while before he manages to look me in the eye again, his cheeks a little flush. "I already found what I like."

I can't fight the smile that stretches across my face. "I can't promise I'm good at relationships."

"I've never been in one before either."

"I found what I like, too," I tell him.

He gives me a lopsided grin. "I'll tell everyone else soon. We can go from there."

"Sounds good. Now come kiss me."

Twenty-Nine

DOMINIC

AS SOON AS our kiss becomes a little heated, moving toward what I hoped would be an amazing blowjob at a minimum, there's a knock on my door.

"Fuck," I curse quietly.

Trevor chuckles, but quickly gets out of the bed and adjusts his cock behind his pants. "Who is it?"

I look through the peephole and spot Jayden.

"It's Jay."

"Oh," he replies, sitting back on the bed.

I open the door and Jayden says, "Have you seen Trevor?"

Taking a step back, I gesture toward the bed. "He's here."

Jayden pokes his head in and laughs. "Y'all motherfuckers are confusing as fuck. Do you hate each other, love each other? Who knows?"

He steps inside so I close the door and head to the other side of the bed. "Already calling it a night?" I ask.

"Yeah, Marcus and Deshawn got shit-faced, tryin' to take shots like they were water. Me and Shea got them back to their rooms. They got babysitters, so don't worry." He takes a breath and moves to sit on the chair near the window. "So, since y'all are back together or whatever the hell this is, can we talk about next weekend? Or will y'all be off again by then?"

Me and Trevor laugh. "We're gonna be fine," he says, which has Jayden's eyebrows raising, and my smile growing.

Another knock interrupts us before we can move onto the plans for Trevor's birthday. When I pull the door open, Dex is on the other side.

"Hey. So this is where the party's at."

I snort. "Hardly a party."

Dex walks in. "I see pizza."

"Have at it."

"Deshawn is throwing his guts up," he says, right before taking a bite. "Not sure if he's gonna be able to play off the hangover he's definitely gonna have in the morning."

"Marcus, too," Jay adds. "Dumbasses."

"You got plans for next Saturday?" Trevor asks Dex.

He shakes his head. "Nah, I don't think so. Why?"

"Birthday plans," Jay says with a grin. "Trev's gonna be the big two one. We're gonna head back to Toast, for sure. Get him on that damn bull," he adds with a laugh. "And I don't know, what do you think about going to Lily Pad?"

"What's that?" I ask.

"It's a gay bar," Jay replies. "But I mainly wanted to ask you, because you're like the only straight," he tells Dex. The pause that follows feels eternal, but he adds. "Well, and Trevor. But you know, me, Ronan, Renzo, Dom..." He lets the sentence trail off before looking at Trevor. "You good with that too, or?"

Dex, completely and one-hundred percent oblivious, says, "I'm cool with it," before biting off another huge chunk of pizza.

"Yeah, me too," Trevor adds before sitting up. "Umm." He rubs his hands together, and I settle in because I already know what he's about to do. "Dex, I gotta tell you something."

Dex spins away from the TV, his eyes focusing on Trevor. "What's up?"

Mine and Jay's eyes are bouncing from each other to the two of them.

Trevor eyes me, studying my face before his lips curl into a small smile. When he looks back at Dex, he says, "I'm gay." Dex was about to take another bite, but his arms slowly drop down as his shell-shocked face is frozen on Trevor. Before he says anything, Trevor adds, "And me and Dominic kinda have a thing going on."

Dex's confused eyes fall to me, then he looks to Jay before focusing on Trevor again. "Um." He laughs a little. "Is this a joke?"

Trevor shakes his head. "Nope. I can tell you the whole, long story if you want, but it basically boils down to me never feeling right when I was with girls, and knowing I found certain guys attractive, but not putting it together that I was gay. Then when things started becoming a little clearer, I just did what I could to keep from admitting it."

"Like getting drunk and making out with a handful of girls," Jay adds.

"Right," Trevor says, shaking his head. "And Renzo and I had a minor little thing a while back. That really brought me around."

Dex makes a noise that's a mix of disbelief and a laugh. "What? Are you fucking with me? You and Renzo?"

His furrowed brows find Jay who just shrugs. "Renzo pulls 'em all. The gays, the straights, the sister's boyfriends, the friends. I don't fucking know."

I laugh at that, but Trevor keeps talking to him. "It was before he was with Ronan, and it wasn't a big deal. I mean, it was, but only because it really solidified things for me, but it was a drunken thing and we didn't allow it to ruin our friendship."

Dex just shakes his head. "I'm just...I don't know what I am. Is this what you meant when you said we all have secrets? This is why you didn't say anything to Zo when you found out about me and Vi?"

Trevor nods. "It wasn't my place. You were gonna tell him when you were ready, just like I was gonna tell people when I was ready."

"Well, wow." He looks at me. "You two, huh?"

I nod, chuckling. "That's a whole different story."

He nods. "Cool." A brief pause as he looks at everyone. "So, we're hitting the clubs next weekend?"

As Jay starts talking to him, I walk around the bed and bend down and place a kiss on Trevor's lips as I cradle his face. "You're making me feel things."

He grins. "Good."

Thirty

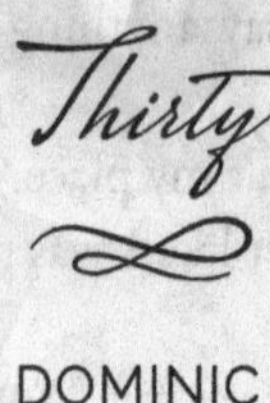

DOMINIC

TURNS OUT, Coach found out about Deshawn and Marcus and their excessive drinking, because they were both throwing up on the plane ride out. Both have been punished by being suspended from the next few games. Which means, me and Trevor get to play on the field together for at least the next few weeks.

I asked for this weekend off, knowing I was going to spend it with Trevor for his birthday, plus we have a home game tonight.

Mom got the insurance money from Dad's death and put half of it toward the mortgage on the house, saving the rest for bills and such until she can find a job. She seems to be doing better each day, and even made friends with another neighbor.

Everything seems to be going really well. Suspiciously well. I feel like I'm waiting for something to ruin it all, but maybe that's just because I'm used to not having a good streak for too long. Anytime me and Mom were doing all right, Dad would show back up or get drunk and ruin the calm and fun environment we had going on.

"Hey, Mom," I say, coming down the hall.

"In the kitchen."

I take a seat at the dining room table where I can watch her spin from the sink to the stove as she cooks something that smells amazing.

"Can I talk to you about something?"

Her brows dip in the center as she takes a towel and wipes her hands. After turning the burner down, she comes and sits across from me. "What's wrong?"

I grin. "Nothing's wrong. I just wanted to talk to you real quick."

"Okay."

"You remember that guy I was telling you about?"

Her face relaxes before her lips curl into a grin. "Yeah."

"He was the one I was with when I saw you out shopping."

"I wondered," she said. "He's cute."

My eyes find the table as I smile. "Yeah. Well, I guess we're a little more serious now."

"Yeah? Is he out now?"

"To his parents and a handful of friends."

"That's good," she says with a nod.

"He told his parents about me. And our friends know, too."

Her smile grows wide. "I'm happy to hear that. He must think a lot of you."

"I don't know why."

"Oh stop."

I shrug, meeting her gaze. "I just wanted you to know about him, because I'll probably be staying at his place this weekend. It's his birthday and we're all going out and celebrating." I pause, feeling weird because I've never talked to my parents about anybody I was with. Granted, it was never serious with anyone until now, but still. "And uhh, he's coming over to pick me up for the game, so if you want to meet him. I mean, officially. Then you can."

Mom rushes over and wraps her arms around my neck, her cheek resting on the top of my head. "I'm so happy for you. Of course I want to meet him." I chuckle, holding her around her waist until she pulls back and holds my face. "I'm happy you're happy."

"Me too."

I hear a door close outside, letting me know Trevor's arrived. My heart beats faster as I stand up and walk to the living room. Introducing him to mom in the capacity of my boyfriend is a huge, unfamiliar step.

His knock comes a second before I reach for the door-knob. He's dressed in jeans and his football jersey, his hair falling across his forehead before he shoves a hand through it, pushing it back.

He grins, taking a deep breath. "Hey."

I feel calmer just looking at him. "Hey. You ready?"

He nods once, rubbing his hands down the sides of his jeans like he's ridding them of sweat.

"Mom," I call, closing the door. She pops out of the kitchen with a huge smile. "This is Trevor." I study his face. "My boyfriend."

His eyes widen slightly. Not because it's new information, but because it's the first time either of us has addressed the other one with the label. He turns to my mom and grins, lifting a hand. "Hi, it's nice to meet you."

He barely has time to get the sentence out before Mom rushes to him and pulls him into a hug. "It's so nice to meet you, too."

Trevor looks at me over her head before lightly wrapping his arms around her. I laugh and shake my head.

Mom steps back, pushing a lock of dark hair over her

shoulder. "Sorry. I'm so happy my son has found someone he wants to introduce me to. You must be very special."

Trevor blushes.

"Well, I guess we should head out," I tell her, picking up my duffle bag. I'll be back Sunday, but let me know if you need anything."

"I'll be fine. You two have fun, but be careful, and good luck with your game. Oh, did you want to take some food with you? I made pozole. I can put it in a tupperware dish."

"It'll just sit in the car for hours while we play," I tell her. "But thanks."

"Next time, then," she says with a smile. "You'll come back for dinner?" She aims the question at Trevor.

"Oh. Yes, I'd love to."

"Good," she replies, still smiling.

As we walk to his car, I grab his hand and squeeze. "We both survived."

He laughs. "She seems really nice."

I lean in and kiss him before we split up and get into the car. "Well, let's win this game so we have something to celebrate later."

He starts the car up. "And if we lose?"

"We console each other with our naked bodies, of course."

"Of course," he says with a snort.

We hold hands all the way to the school and nothing's ever felt better.

Thirty-One

TREVOR

WE END up winning our game, both of us scoring a touchdown, and our team winning by ten. So far, we're undefeated, but we have plenty of games to go. While some of the team wants to go out and party, most of us decide to do our own thing considering we have a full night planned ahead of us for tomorrow. Dex and Vi go on a date, Jay says he's gonna find someone to hang out with, and me and Dom share a look, knowing we'll be together at my place tonight.

"Guess we have a reason to celebrate," he says with a wide grin as he climbs into my car.

"Yeah. What do you wanna do? Drink champagne? Gorge ourselves on junk food?" I tease, fastening my seatbelt.

He moves quickly, leaning over the console and grabbing my face. "You know exactly what we're gonna do." His eyes drop to my mouth as his thumb grazes my bottom lip. "Don't you?"

Our gazes connect and I nod, already entranced.

"Tell me what we're gonna do, Campbell. Just so I know there's no confusion." His lips pull up slightly.

"We're gonna have sex."

His eyebrows shoot up as his head cocks to the side. "Oh, are we?"

We've only had sex the one time when he rode me. I've been preparing myself to be able to take him, and I think I'm finally ready. There's only so much toys can do anyway.

I nod. "I want you to fuck me."

His face changes, and the only way I can explain the look in his eyes is hunger. He looks at me like he can't wait to devour me, and I'm eager to be consumed.

He mashes his lips against mine before pulling away. "Well, let's not waste another second."

His hand rests on my thigh the entire ride home while he teases me with vulgar words that create filthy promises.

Once we make it to my house, my cock is already hard and ready to burst free from my pants. Having already showered after the game, we don't have to worry about taking the time to do that, so once inside, we head directly to the room, and that's where Dominic takes over.

We face each other and he takes several seconds to allow his eyes to roam my body from head to toe.

"I want to throw you on the bed and fuck you and claim you, and make sure you never forget what I feel like." He exhales a long harsh breath. "But I don't want to hurt you either."

"You won't hurt me," I tell him, even though I'm not completely certain about that.

He steps forward and runs his hands under my shirt, feeling on my stomach and chest before gripping the hem and ripping it over my head. I kick off my shoes while he does the same, and watch as he removes his shirt and tosses it to the floor with mine.

With dexterous fingers, he undoes my pants without a hitch, his hands sliding in and cupping my ass before he shoves the material to the floor, leaving me in just a gray pair of boxer-briefs.

"Fuck, Trevor," he breathes, reaching out and grazing a finger over my cock before touching the wet spot that was created by my arousal. "You're so fucking perfect." He removes his pants and underwear, his erection springing free. "Get on your knees and let me see those perfect lips around my cock."

I drop down, touching his thighs and gazing up at him. He runs his fingers through my hair, keeping a grip on the strands as he guides himself into my mouth. I moan as I take him to the throat.

"Fuck." He drags the word out, watching his dick slide between my lips. Letting go of his shaft, he says, "Suck my dick, baby. Show me how much you love it."

My heart does a somersault at the term of endearment, and my cock twitches with the command. I take over, stroking, licking and sucking like my life depends on it. I make him moan and cuss and tug on my hair, driving him wild.

When he can't take it anymore, he yanks me up, devouring my mouth with his tongue as he walks us to the bed. I drop down on my back and wait for him to pounce.

"Take them off," he says, eyeing my boxer-briefs.

Once they're on the floor, he crawls on the bed and takes me into his mouth. "Christ," he murmurs, releasing me briefly. "I could taste you all day and never get tired of it."

I moan, my back arching. "Taste it," I whisper. "Stroke it. Do whatever you want, just don't stop touching me."

His response is a low and sexy growl before he takes my cock into his mouth again, skillfully bringing me to the brink of an orgasm in minutes. When he pulls away, I groan.

"Think I'm letting you come already? We're just getting started."

He leaves me on the bed and goes to my nightstand where he pulls out some lube, and one of the two toys I now have.

"Turn over. On your knees, so I can see that tight ass I'm about to drive into."

Dominic wastes no time getting behind me, his hands on my ass cheeks, spreading me open before his tongue darts out and licks a surprisingly gentle path up and down.

"Holy shit," I breathe, fisting the covers.

He moans, focusing on my hole. His tongue circles it before attempting to push inside. After a few minutes he backs away, but he's not gone long. His lubed up finger slides inside me, making me gasp and moan.

"Yeah, you like that, don't you?" he asks.

"I love it."

It doesn't take long for him to move onto the toy, making sure it's coated liberally with the lube before attempting to push it in. His body moves to my side, allowing him to control the toy with his right hand while being able to grab my face with his left.

"Once you're comfortable with this, you'll get my dick. You gonna be able to take it?"

I bite my lip, my entire body on fire from the inside out. "Yes."

"Such a good boy," he croons, kissing me before focusing on fucking me with the toy.

It's nearly ten minutes later when I feel like I might die if I don't get more. He's done such a good job giving me enough to get used to the feeling, but not enough to send me over the edge.

"Dominic, please," I beg. "I need you. I need more."

"Mm. Say that first part again."

"I need you."

He carefully removes the toy before saying, "Turn over. I

want you on your back so I can look in your eyes when I'm inside you."

I get up on my knees, ready to move, but when Dominic looks at my dick, I follow his gaze. Pre-cum drips from my crown, and there's a small amount of wetness on my comforter.

"Looks like you made a mess," he muses, pressing his fingers to the liquid. "So ready for my cock, aren't you?"

I lay on my back, staring at him with hooded eyes as I stroke my length. "You know I am."

Knowing we were gonna get to this point, we both already got tested. So no condom's needed— something we're both happy about.

Dominic reaches for the lube, slathering a good amount on his cock before squirting more in his hand. On his knees, he moves forward, his hand slipping between my cheeks, coating my entrance before his fingers slide in.

"Oh yeah. You're ready."

"Stop teasing and fuck me already."

His lips quirk up. "But I love how desperate you are."

"You'll love how tight I am even more, I think," I say, arching a brow and tugging on my cock. "But I can get there on my own if you won't help."

He knocks my hand away. "You're gonna come with me inside you or not at all. I've been waiting for this for way too long."

With his dick in one hand and the other pushing one of my legs up, he guides himself in slowly. His crown breeches the tight ring of muscle and I groan as I squeeze his bicep.

"Oh God."

"Look at me." At his command, I realize my eyes are squeezed tight. When I open them and meet his gaze, he says, "I know it seems like I'm in control, but it's you. Tell me to stop and I'll stop."

I nod. "Keep going." He gets his crown inside me and air rushes from my lungs. He's much wider than any toy I have, but I want this. Need this. "More."

Dominic pushes in, giving me every inch, but takes his time getting there. Once he's buried to the hilt, he drops his head. "Jesus Christ."

He leans over me, his body sliding across mine as he rocks in and out. "Fuck, you're so big."

His chuckle is low. "Just now realizing?"

"Shut up and keep moving."

His mouth brushes against my neck, kissing a path up to my cheek before finding my mouth. I grab his face and slide my tongue across his, kissing him with the same fire that burns through my body.

This position gives us more intimacy. I'm able to wrap my arms around him while he kisses my face and neck, grunting sounds of pleasure while I moan into his shoulder with each thrust.

"Fuck, Trevor. I can't wait to have you in every way possible. You feel too good."

An erotic moan leaves my mouth, but I can't think clearly enough to form any coherent thoughts or sexy statements. The truth is, it feels too good to even talk about. How can I tell him that this moment is the best sexual experience in my life? How can I describe this feeling of being so overwhelmed with desire, I can't imagine it ever ending? I want him inside me forever.

"Don't stop," is all I manage to get out, but it's enough.

Dominic lets loose a sexy, animalistic growl and picks up the pace a little more. Getting up on his knees, he holds my legs up and watches as his cock moves in and out of me. He bites down on his bottom lip before his gaze travels to my face.

"I'm never gonna get enough of this. Your ass..." his eyes move back down as he thrusts harder and deeper. "Your ass is mine now. There's no way I'm letting anyone else get close to this."

I sink my teeth into my lip as I try to keep from smiling too wide. "Good. I don't want anyone else."

His hips move faster as he shifts around, getting us both at an angle where his cock reaches deep inside me. Stars explode in my eyes when he hits that spot.

"Oh God, Dominic."

"Yeah," he growls.

He keeps going, skillfully tapping on my prostate with each thrust inside.

Unexplainable bliss travels through my entire body and I frantically seek something to hold onto.

"Dominic," I whimper.

"Yes, baby," he moans. "You ready to come for me?" I'm only able to nod. "Stroke your cock and make a mess for me. Let me see just how much you enjoy my dick in your ass."

"Oh, I fucking love it," I say, grabbing my erection and sliding my hand up and down.

Only a couple minutes later, I feel the orgasm building. Dominic's movements are on fast forward as sweat makes his skin glisten.

"Fuck, Trevor," he grunts. "I'm so close, baby."

I moan. "Me too."

"Let me see it," he says, eyeing my cock.

"Oh shit," I cry out as warm, white ribbons of cum shoot out and land on my stomach.

"Fuck yes." His voice is low and raspy.

"Oh my God," I breathe, still sucking in breaths and twitching with the aftershocks of the most powerful orgasm of my life.

Before I can even get my bearings, Dominic is grunting and rocking into me with a furious pace. "Oh fuck. Oh, God."

He comes deep inside me, roaring into the room.

"I...I don't know..." I take a breath, taking my hand off my cock, looking at the mess on my thumb.

Dominic reaches for my wrist and brings my hand to his mouth, licking the residue from my skin. "So fucking good."

I flop back, my body completely spent and everything feeling like Jell-O. "God, you're so good."

He slowly and gently eases out of me. "And to think you hated me."

I open my eyes to look at him. "I never hated you."

His lips twitch before he comes around the side of me, leaning down to kiss me. "I know you didn't."

I'm so far from hating him at this moment, it takes everything in me not to say something I'm not even sure is true yet. Maybe sex is making me stupid. Do I...? No. It's too early to have strong feelings, isn't it?

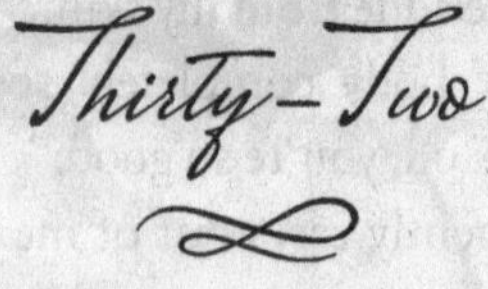

Thirty-Two

TREVOR

HOW IS it possible to feel this happy simply by being around another human being? This morning, I woke up in an extremely good mood, thanks to the life altering sex I had last night, followed by hours of talking, touching, and cuddling.

The morning blowjob I received and performed helped as well. Dominic says we should wait at least a day before we have sex again, since I am sore, but if he thinks I'm celebrating my birthday tonight and not having sex, he's wrong.

I hear a crash from the kitchen as I'm sitting on the couch in the living room. "Do you need some help?"

"No. Stay in there," he says. "Shit," he murmurs, probably having hurt himself. "I'm almost done."

I grin, shaking my head before I glance over my shoulder to see what he's doing. He told me he'd make me breakfast since it's my birthday, but he didn't tell me whether he has a lot of experience cooking or not. Based on the amount of times he's cussed, and/or dropped things, I'm going to assume not a lot.

After a few more minutes of me pretending to watch TV

but instead watching him struggle to find everything he needs, he calls out to me.

"Okay, you can come in now."

I push up from the couch and head over, spotting a couple of plates with scrambled eggs, sausage, bacon, and tortillas. On another plate is a couple pieces of toast and next to it are two cups of orange juice.

His eyes bounce from the plates to my face, looking a bit happy with himself, but also worried. "What do you think?"

"Looks good," I tell him. "How many times did you burn yourself?"

"Let's not talk about that," he says, glancing at his hand. "I didn't know if you wanted toast or not. I wrap all my food up in tortillas, but I made both. And you can't have breakfast without orange juice."

"Thank you," I say with a smile, rounding the island to wrap my arm around him. "I appreciate this."

He kisses my temple. "Happy birthday. Let's hope it's edible."

The food is definitely good. We both scarf down everything fairly quickly.

"I may need you to make me some more meals," I tease as I sit back in my chair.

He scoffs. "Maybe we shouldn't risk that. Also, how do people crack eggs without getting shells in the pan? I had to scoop out like six fucking pieces."

I laugh, getting up to take the plates to the sink. "Feel free to come over every morning to perfect your egg cracking skills."

"I'd prefer using some of my other skills."

"Oh yeah? You have other skills?"

He rushes up behind me, wrapping his arms around me as he playfully bites my neck. I laugh, nearly dropping the dishes.

"Want me to bend you over this sink and show you?"

"Mm." I bite my lip. "Think I'd say no to that?"

"So you *are* aware of my skills."

"I hate you."

He kisses my cheek before stepping away and sitting on the counter next to me. "I thought we went over this last night."

"It's a love/hate sort of thing," I say before freezing, my eyes widening as I stare into the sink. That's not really what I meant to say. It just came out, but hopefully he doesn't think this is me revealing my feelings. "Or just hate," I add, turning the water on and avoiding his gaze. "You are pretty annoying."

"Yeah, *I'm* the annoying one," he teases, allowing me to breathe a sigh of relief.

"So what do you want to do while we wait to head out tonight?" I ask.

He looks at his watch. "Well, we have about eight hours. You sure you won't get sick of me?"

I allow my eyes to travel up and down his body. "I'm pretty sure."

"You want me?" he asks with a grin. "Because I'll spend all goddamn day in bed with you if that's what you want. You're the birthday boy."

"I thought you said we should wait to have sex?"

"Nobody said anything about sex, you little fiend."

I roll my eyes. "If I'm the birthday boy, I should get whatever I want."

He arches a brow. "Oh? You gonna tell me what you want?"

"You already know."

"I want you to tell me. In detail."

I drop the dishes and shut off the water, taking a second to dry my hands before I walk over and step between his legs, my hands slowly traveling up his thighs before grabbing onto his hips. My lips brush against his cheek before I nuzzle my face into his neck, my tongue darting out to lick a small patch of skin under his ear.

With my lips near his ear, I say, "Maybe later." Then I step away and smirk at him.

"I hate you," he groans.

"Oh yeah?"

He jumps down, pushing me against the counter and trapping me between his arms. "Hating you is damn near impossible. The opposite, though..." he trails off, his forehead leaning against mine before he pushes his lips to mine.

He never finishes his thought because we get too wrapped up in each other.

"How are we doing this tonight?" he questions as we're getting ready to leave.

"What do you mean?"

"Well, we're...together?" He forms it like a question as he studies me with an arched brow.

My tongue swipes across my lip as I grin. "We're together," I confirm.

"But only a handful of people know, and we're gonna be around most of the team tonight, so I'm assuming we're just keeping it friendly."

"I guess just normal."

"Normal was you acting like you hated my guts when really you just wanted to be in my pants."

I roll my eyes. "Okay, I won't pretend I hate you. I just won't kiss you, or touch you, or..." I drag my gaze down his body, loving how his shirt fits snug across his shoulders and how his ass looks in those jeans.

"Eye fuck me?" He laughs. "Good luck with that."

"Let me just get it out of the way now," I say, stepping up

to him and melding my lips against his as my hand grabs his ass.

The kiss turns fiery and I'm all but grinding against him as my breaths come in heavy pants.

"Now you're just turning us both on," he says, pulling away. "If you think I won't lure you into a bathroom and shove my cock down your throat, you're dead wrong."

I bite my lip. "Maybe I'd like that."

He laughs. "Come on, Campbell. We're late to your own birthday party."

Knowing we're both planning on getting pretty drunk, we get an Uber to drive us to the first bar of the night—Toast. Jay's already texted me asking where the hell we were, so I assume everyone else is already inside.

"Gonna try to ride the bull tonight?" Dom asks, his lips curling up on one side.

"Uh, no. I'm not good at riding..." The rest of the sentence dies on my tongue, because amusement twinkles in his eyes as his smile grows.

"I think we can find out if that's true soon enough."

I feel my cheeks heat up. "Stop."

A few seconds later, we're inside the club and pushing through groups of people, searching for our friends.

"There," Dominic says, pointing at the bar.

When we approach, a chorus of *Happy Birthdays* ring out before Jay says, "Okay, shots!"

I snort, and everybody crowds the bar, ordering shots and putting them on their open tabs. There's about six guys from the team, not including Jay and Dex, plus Ronan and Renzo, and Jay's friends, Olivia and Bryant. We're a pretty good sized group, so once we get our shots and a round of drinks ordered, we head away from the bar and find a table that'll only fit five of us. Not many are planning to stay seated anyway, so it works out.

"To Trevor, the nicest guy I know," Jay says, holding up his glass, his eyes dancing to everyone else. "No offense."

Renzo rolls his eyes. "Happy birthday, man. Here's to you. We all love you and hope you have the best fucking night you'll never remember."

"Fuck yeah!" a few people yell.

Everyone raises their shot glasses before swallowing down the liquid. The rum burns a path down my throat and warms my chest.

"I wish I could lick the taste of that rum from your tongue," Dominic whispers as he reaches across me to grab his drink.

"You're killing me," I groan.

He smirks.

During the course of the next few hours, everyone takes their turn on the dancefloor or attempting to ride that damn mechanical bull. I laughed my ass off when Renzo's cocky ass thought he would be able to hold on, but was thrown off several seconds in.

A few of the single guys have found girls to dance with, and I think Marcus actually left with someone already. I'm not a big dancer, but what am I gonna do? Dance with a girl I'm not interested in while Dominic watches? No thanks. He's also kept off the dancefloor, even though I've noticed a guy in here watching him who'd be more than happy to take him for a spin.

"That fucking guy is still looking at you," I say as we're watching Jay attempt to ride the bull.

Dominic snorts, his head angling to the side to find who I'm talking about. "The one in the stripes?"

"Yep."

He looks back at me, his lips pulled into a grin. "I'm not interested in him, though."

I shake my head, fighting a smile. The more I drink, the

more handsy I wanna be with him. I've had to force myself to leave his side, because otherwise people are gonna think it's weird we're so close all of a sudden.

Once Jay falls off the bull, he comes outside the pen, laughing. "I swear to God that guy turns that thing up on me more than anyone else."

Dex laughs. "No he doesn't."

"Wanna head to Lily Pad soon?" he asks us.

I shrug. "Sure."

"We're going to Lily Pad?" Shea asks.

"Yeah." Jay looks at his watch. "In half an hour or so. You guys don't gotta come," he says, aiming the statement at the straight guys on the team. "But some of us want to."

"I don't really care," Shea says. "My girlfriend can't come out tonight, and at a gay bar, at least there's less of a chance for me to be stupid and fuck up my relationship."

Liv chimes in. "Ugh. I hate men. How about you just not be stupid. You have to be around people who aren't interested in you to not cheat?"

Jay laughs. "Less of a chance, so there's still a chance you could be stupid at a gay bar. I mean, you are a lot of gay guys' type," he teases.

Shea flips everyone off before heading to the table.

The group gathers around the table, drinking the rest of our drinks while several of us order Ubers to take us to Lily Pad.

The guy in stripes approaches Dominic, and I watch from the other side of the circle, completely surprised at the balls he has to come up to him while he's around so many of us.

Most people don't notice, but my heart rate spikes as I watch him touch Dominic's arm to get his attention. Dom's eyes flash to mine briefly before he bends down a little to hear what the guy has to say.

I can't hear him from here, but I know he's kept his hand

on Dominic's arm and has gotten a little too close to his body for my liking.

Renzo and Jay get my attention. Renzo's brows are furrowed as he jerks his head in Dom's direction, basically telling me to step in. Jay's wide eyes bounce between us. More people have noticed Mr. Stripes talking to Dominic. Fucking Tim mutters something about Dom being able to get some tonight.

I watch Dom shake his head slightly, giving this guy a polite smile. He's probably trying to let him down easy, but this guy grabs his hand and tugs it near his cock.

The fucking audacity.

I storm across the circle and break the grip he has on Dominic's hand, scowling at the guy in stripes. "He's with me," I say between gritted teeth.

His brows raise in surprise, and he lifts his hands in defeat before he spins around and leaves. I look up at Dominic who's watching me with a shocked and somewhat amused expression.

I slowly turn my head and find every set of eyes on us. Guess I made a bigger scene than I thought. I didn't even think about what I was doing, but I was not about to have this random guy try to make Dominic touch his dick. Even if most of them couldn't hear what I said, the action in itself says enough.

I slip my hand in Dominic's and turn to face him. His eyes search mine, asking if I know what the hell I'm doing. I slide my other hand across his jaw and press my lips against his.

It's not a long kiss, just a simple peck, but it gets the message across.

I face the sea of confused, shocked, and few happy faces. In a loud voice, I say, "Yes, I'm gay, and me and Dominic are together."

Eyes seek out other eyes, wondering if they heard it right. Dominic squeezes my hand.

"I'm gonna assume most of you don't have a problem with that," Dom says. "But if you do, you can get the fuck over it."

Jay laughs. "That's what I'm saying."

After a few more seconds of silence, Shea says, "Man, whatever. Just as long as y'all can still win us some football games."

Deshawn shrugs. "Don't matter to me. Not my business."

"Cars are here," Dex announces.

"Let's go," I say, and Dominic drapes a heavy arm over my shoulders as we walk out.

"You're doing it again," he mutters.

"What's that?"

"Making me feel things."

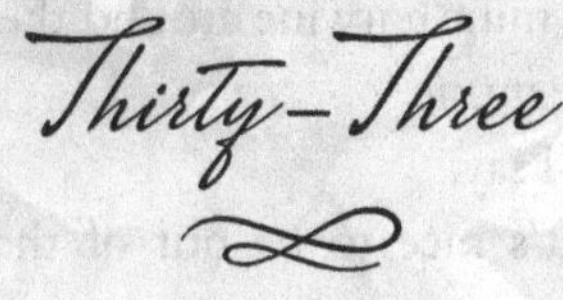

Thirty-Three

TREVOR

LILY PAD IS NEARLY AS PACKED as Toast was, but in here you see more same-sex pairings, and to be honest, it's a nice sight.

Like at Toast, the first thing we all do is order a bunch of shots, then people spread out—either heading to the dance-floor, or finding a table to sit at. And since everybody knows about me and Dominic now, we're able to sit next to each other and touch like any other couple.

When a sultry slow song comes on, Dominic leans over and whispers in my ear, "Wanna dance?"

I jolt back and look him in the eye to see if he's serious. "For real?"

He holds my gaze. "Why not?"

My eyes bounce around. It's not like we'd be the only same-sex couple slow dancing, but I guess I'm still trying to break the chains that keep me tied to other people's opinions. The guys on the team are here, and even though they know and didn't react negatively, I guess there's still a fear of judgement.

"Come on, Campbell," he says, grabbing my hand. "It's just me and you. Don't worry about anyone else."

I go with him, sliding out of the booth and following him to the other side of the dancefloor. He wraps his arms around my waist and I let mine entwine around the back of his neck, and we sway to the music.

"This is nice," I say.

He smirks. "It's nice to be out of that head of yours, isn't it?"

"Even better to be with you."

His lips push against mine in a quick kiss. It's nothing too passionate, but kissing him in public feels so good, especially when I don't have to be concerned about how others might react. It's freeing to be with him like this without a worry in the world. It may have something to do with the fact that I'm finally embracing who I am, but I think it has a lot to do with how comfortable he makes me feel. With him, I don't feel like I have to worry at all.

"What're you thinking about?" he asks.

"Hmm?"

"You're grinning."

I laugh. "I'm happy."

"It's because of me, huh?" he says with a smirk.

I roll my eyes, but don't bother denying it.

When the song ends, he pulls me close and rests his forehead against mine. "I'm happy because of you, too."

The rest of the night is filled with lots of drinking, games being played at our tables, an embarrassingly loud rendition of the Happy Birthday song being sung to me by my drunk friends, and so much laughter my cheeks will likely hurt for days.

Right before last call, Dominic tells me he's gonna go to the bathroom while I call for an Uber. We're both pretty tipsy, as is everyone else in our group, but even if I feel like shit tomorrow, it will be worth it.

I say bye to my friends and thank them for hanging out with me tonight, then I head to the bathroom before Dominic has a chance to leave.

When I'm inside, I make sure nobody else is here and then lock the door. Dom looks at me over his shoulder as he's washing his hands, a crooked grin on his lips.

"You just gonna stand there and stare at me?" he asks, mimicking what he told me the first time I met him in the bathroom of his frat.

I smile. "Maybe."

He shuts the water off and grabs some paper towels to dry his hands before turning and facing me. "I think you should do more than that."

I march toward him, knowing I don't have much time to waste. I unfasten his jeans and drop to my knees to take him into my mouth.

"Holy shit," he gasps, reaching for my head.

I suck him until he hardens in my mouth. When he starts thrusting, I back away and stand up, giving him a smirk. "You can finish in my ass when we get home."

His lips part as he takes his cock in his hand. "Oh, you're evil."

"I'm the birthday boy, remember? I get what I want."

"It's technically not your birthday anymore," he says, stroking his length and making my eyes travel to his action.

"Are you gonna deny me?" I ask, meeting his gaze again and wetting my bottom lip with a swipe of my tongue.

"Never."

～

It feels like it takes forever to get to my house, but that's probably just because I'm horny as fuck, and Dominic keeps teasing me in the back seat of this Uber.

Once we pull up to the house, I pay the driver and add an extra large tip before all but running through the front door. After a quick trip to the bathroom, where I hurriedly wash down the intimate parts of my body, and leave only my boxer-briefs on, I head straight to my bedroom only to be disappointed that Dominic isn't here.

I spin around and find him coming through the bedroom door, probably having just used the other bathroom down the hall.

I bite my lip, anxious to be with him.

"You sure you're not too sore?" he asks from the doorway.

"Positive."

"Good. Get that toy I bought you."

My nostrils flare as heat spreads throughout my body. Dominic bought a dildo that has a suction cup on the end. It's smaller than he is, but he said he had a reason, and I guess I'm about to find out what it is.

I grab the dildo and some lube and wait for him to tell me what to do next. He pads across the floor, taking the toy from my hand. "Squirt some lube on it. Stroke it really well and make sure it's coated."

I do as he says. "What are we gonna do?"

"You'll see."

He secures the dildo to my wooden floor, and then pushes my underwear down and bends me over the bed.

I gasp as his hands spread my cheeks and his tongue licks the space between them. "Oh, God."

Dominic tongues my ass, bringing me an insane amount of pleasure in such a short time. After a few minutes, he coats his fingers in lube and slides them into my ass.

"You ready to ride that cock?"

"I want your cock," I breathe.

"You'll get it soon enough."

When I start pushing back on his fingers, he removes them and pulls me to a standing position. He drops his boxers and strokes himself.

"Sit on that cock while you suck mine."

A thrill of excitement runs through me. "Okay."

His lips curl up on both ends. "Good boy."

I've learned to love that term of endearment. It makes my stomach clench.

With a squirt of lube on my hand, I coat myself and stroke the dildo before getting into position and slowly sliding down the shaft.

"Oh God," I moan.

"Mm. That's it, baby," he says, watching closely.

I'm on my knees as I take it all the way in, bouncing up and down a little. Dominic stands in front of me and I open my mouth, letting him slide his dick between my lips and across my tongue.

"Oh fuck," he groans. "You look so fucking perfect right now."

My eyes flick up at him as I hold onto his thighs and moan around his length.

"Hold on tight, baby," he says before his hips start moving faster, his cock fucking my mouth with desperate fervor.

My fingers press into his muscled thighs as I hold onto him for balance while also moving enough to get pleasure out of the silicone cock in my ass.

When I gag, he pulls back, giving me time to recuperate before continuing.

"I could fuck your mouth all night," he moans, his eyes closed as he drops his head back, his pace slower. "You feel so good." After a few more pumps into my mouth, he pulls out and looks down at me. "But your ass is better."

I move slowly, and when the toy slips out, I get to my feet and he attacks my mouth with a wildly passionate kiss, our tongues twirling around each other as our hands roam one another's body.

Dominic pulls away first, snatching the lube up and coating himself and me with the clear liquid before bending me over the side of the mattress again. This time he lifts one of my legs up until my knee rests on the bed, leaving me spread open for him.

With a hand gripping my shoulder, he guides himself in, and thanks to the toy, it's a faster process to slip past the ring of muscle.

He teases me with slow movements, not giving me all of him right away. His hands rub my ass cheeks before rounding my hips and traveling up my back.

"Fuck me," I beg.

"You need it, don't you? You need my cock to make you feel good."

"Yes," I pant, not caring how desperate I sound. "I need it. Please."

"Mm," he moans. "Say it again."

"Please, Dominic."

He lets loose then, gripping my waist firmly, moving in and out with unbridled thrusts. He grunts and pants like an animal, but fuck it turns me on.

"Yes!" I cry out. "Fuck me. Oh God, it feels so good."

He plants one of his feet on the mattress and it seems to give him the ability to move deeper and harder. His hands move to my shoulders, holding onto me while he pummels inside, making me feel every fucking inch.

"Fuck, Trevor," he grunts.

I brace myself on my left forearm, taking hold of my cock in my right. "You got me so fucking hard," I pant.

"Stroke it. Come all over the bed while I come in your ass."

It's just a few minutes later when pleasure licks up my spine and my balls draw up tight, every nerve ending in my body tingling with bliss as my orgasm hits and I unleash my load on the comforter.

"Shit!"

My body tightens up, muscles flexing as I come apart, cries of satisfaction leaving my mouth as I try to catch my breath.

"Oh fuck," Dominic says moments later. "Oh God, yes."

Hard and deep thrusts turn a little slower as he hits his own peak of ecstasy. He pushes in deep and stays there and I feel his cock throb inside me as he empties himself.

"Yes," I breathe.

His sweaty forehead touches my back as he nearly collapses on top of me, his body twitching. "Fuck."

"It's so good," I murmur.

"Baby," he whispers. "My God."

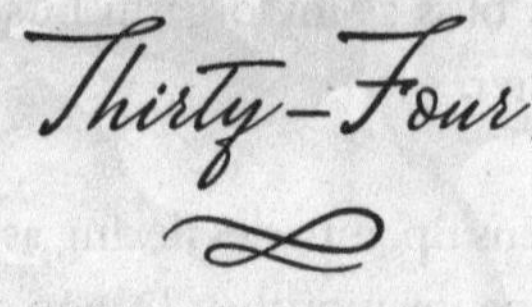

Thirty-Four

DOMINIC

ON MONDAY MORNING, with only a little bit of hesitancy on his part, Trevor and I show up to campus together, hand in hand. A few people glance, but nobody really seems to care. It's not like we're the only gay guys at this school, but I know to Trevor, it probably feels like all eyes are on him.

"This is new to me, too," I tell him.

He makes a face as he looks at me. "Yeah, I'm sure."

I laugh. "I mean, I've never dated anyone, so I've never held hands and done this boyfriend thing."

"Boyfriend thing," he says with a snort. "Don't sound so excited."

I kiss his temple as we approach the quad. "I am excited. I love spending time with you."

He grins, squeezing my hand. "You're not too bad either."

"Oh, whatever. Give me a kiss and go to class. I'll see you later."

He steps forward and presses his lips to mine. "Bye."

"Bye," I reply with a smile before watching him strut off.

I spin around, needing to head in the opposite direction,

and spot Jay passing me. "You all in love now, Hernandez?" he teases.

"Fuck off," I say, the smile still in place as I head to class.

My first two classes seem to drag, but that's because I'm anxious to see Trevor again. Before, I didn't see him until football practice at the end of the day, but now that we're together, I will definitely take the time to meet up with him during lunch.

In the cafeteria, I get in line and spot Trevor entering the room, holding a book at his side. His smile grows when he sees me wave at him, and my heart does something weird in my chest.

He stops next to me and I wrap my arm around his waist and give him a kiss. "I missed you," I say quietly against his lips.

"You spend one weekend with me and now you're obsessed," he jokes, giving me another kiss.

"You spent twenty minutes with me in a bathroom and were obsessed."

"Oh, is that right?"

"I think so."

He rolls his eyes. "Infatuated, maybe."

"I'll take it."

Somebody walking toward us does a double take and then stops next to Trevor. His dark eyes study us while his brows dip in the center. "Trev?"

Trevor turns and faces this guy I don't know. "Oh. Hey."

I sense his nervousness in just those two words.

"You...uhh." His eyes move between us, and I straighten my back and stare at him, waiting to see what he has to say. "It's been a minute. How ya been?"

"I've been good. How about you?"

"Fine. Just struggling to get through this ridiculous European history class." He laughs. "Sienna was asking about you the other day." His eyes jump to me again as we move forward in line.

"Oh yeah? Hope she's doing okay."

"She's fine." He walks backwards to keep up with us as we move ahead, getting our food. He laughs a little. "I'm sorry, but uhh...are you...into guys?"

My eyes find this guy again, wondering if he's trying to hit on him or about to be an asshole. Trevor chuckles lightly.

"I'm into this one," he answers, jerking his head toward me and making my heart do another little flip.

"Oh. I had no idea."

"You're not the only one," Trev says with an easy smile.

"I guess I'll tell Sienna to stop asking about you."

He laughs. "Probably a good idea."

"Well, it was good seeing you."

"You, too."

Once he's gone, and we're able to move through the line and grab our lunch, I take a glance at Trevor. "You handled that well."

"He's an old friend. Well, acquaintance really. We used to have a couple classes together last year. And he's the brother of a girl I may or may not have made out with a few times."

"Ah. I see." I pause. "Kinda want to push you against a wall and shove my tongue down your throat and my hand down your pants."

Trevor laughs. "Why's that?"

"Because you said you were into me."

"But you know that already."

"But you told someone else."

He grabs my waist and kisses my cheek. "I'll tell more people if it makes you want to do things to me."

I bite my lip. "Well, that's nothing new."

"Let's go eat, and maybe we can feel each other up in a bathroom before our next class."

~

We don't get to feel each other up, unfortunately. But the rest of the day moves quickly, and before I know it I'm in the locker room, waiting for Trevor to show up.

Since some of the guys were with us for Trevor's birthday, I know they're aware of Trev's sexuality and our relationship, and maybe they've already told some of the others, but so far, nobody's said anything.

I'm already changed when Trev rushes in, ripping his shirt off. "Got caught up after class talking to my professor," he says as he quickly strips down and puts his practice gear on.

I wait behind with him even as everyone else heads to the field. "Do you think the rest of the team know yet?"

"Probably some. Guys gossip just as much as girls."

"You cool with that, though?"

"I'm not going back in the closet, Dom."

"Okay," I say with a light chuckle.

As soon as he's ready, we jog out and catch up with the team. Luckily a couple other people are running late too, so it doesn't look like we were just fooling around in the locker room.

Once practice is done and we're all back inside, Trevor looks me up and down. "Wanna go home and shower with me?" His cheeks redden and I reach out to caress one with my knuckle.

My smile grows, and I bite my lip, thinking of all the things I can do to him in a shower. I can't get enough of this guy. "I have about two and a half hours before I have to be at work."

"So, yes?"

"Fuck yes."

He kisses me quickly before we start changing. A couple guys walking by saw our brief moment of intimacy.

"Uh. What?"

When Trevor and I turn around, we simply just look at them and wait to see what they're gonna say. Trevor shouldn't have to come out to every person he comes across. If they see us kissing or holding hands, then you can assume we're pretty gay and together, and that should be enough.

One of the guys—Lucas, just shrugs and says, "Okay, then."

"They'll get used to it," I tell him.

"It hasn't been too bad," Trev says. "A couple other people asked me about it in class, having either heard about it from someone or they saw us in the quad in the morning or in the cafeteria. I just confirmed that it was true, but nobody's been hateful."

"That's good."

"Yeah." He smiles.

"I'm gonna call my mom on the way over. She may be out at job interviews, but I'm gonna let her know I'll be home after work."

"Okay."

"Hey, Dom," Dex says, walking up next to me.

"What's up?"

"Not to be nosy, but you said your mom is looking for a job?"

"Yeah, she's trying. Says it hasn't been easy."

Dex nods. I told him a little about my backstory, so he's aware of the situation we're in, and how my mom needs to get a job soon to be able to keep afloat.

"My dad's secretary quit. He's stressing about needing someone to replace her as soon as possible. I don't know what all he's needing her to be able to do, but if I talk to him, I can probably get him to hire your mom."

"Yeah?" I ask, surprised and a little overwhelmed that he'd do that for me. It's not like he's known me for long.

"Of course. To be transparent, my dad is a workaholic and works crazy long hours. I'm not sure what it would be like to work for him."

"Beggars can't be choosers," I say with a shrug. "Let me know what he says and I'll talk to my mom."

"Will do."

"Thanks, man."

Dex nods and leaves.

"You got some good friends here, Campbell."

"Yeah, I got lucky."

I wrap an arm around his shoulders and gaze into his eyes. "Me too."

Thirty-Five

DOMINIC

WEEKS PASS, and everything between me and Trevor keeps getting better and better. I spend so much time at his house, I feel like I should be paying for the utilities at least.

Halloween came and went, and after spending time with my mom, passing out candy, Trevor and I went to a party at Jay's frat. We dressed as Maverick and Iceman from the movie Top Gun, because, come on, we all know those two wanted each other. That movie is ripe with homoeroticism. Trevor didn't want to wear towels like they did in the locker room scene, so flight suits it was.

If people hadn't figured out we were together before the Halloween party, they definitely found out then, because we could hardly keep our hands off each other. Maybe the flight suits weren't a bad idea, because Trevor looked damn good in his.

It's now the middle of November, and we're quickly approaching Thanksgiving break. Mom's already asked me if Trevor will join us, but I've yet to ask him. I know his parents always have something, so I don't want to put him in a hard spot.

"Hey, I have a question for you," he says, coming from around the back of the couch and dropping next to me with a bowl of popcorn.

"Okay." I take a few pieces and toss them in my mouth as I pull Netflix up on the TV.

"Thanksgiving."

I angle my head and study him. "What about it?"

"I was wondering if after you spend time with your mom, if you wanted to come to my parents house?"

I remove my feet from the coffee table and plant them on the floor, shifting to face him. "You want me to meet your parents?"

"Is that weird? I've met your mom."

"Yeah, I know. It's not weird at all. I guess I just wasn't expecting that. My mom was actually asking if you were gonna come to our house," I say with a laugh.

"Oh really?"

"Think we can eat two Thanksgiving dinners?"

He grins. "I think we can manage."

"So a holiday with the parents. Are we growing up?"

With a snort, he says, "I hope not."

Thanksgiving day arrives and the knots in my stomach make me feel like I won't be able to eat anything at all. I'm not nervous about him coming to eat with me and my mom. We've all been together on a few occasions, but meeting his parents is another story. I've never met someone's parents before. What if they don't like me? What if they're not really okay with their son being gay? So many *what ifs*.

The plan is to eat here at my place with my mom first since she gets up hella early to start cooking and the food will be ready by noon. His parents plan to have food ready around six.

"When's he gonna be here?" Mom asks from her place in front of the stove.

"He texted me before he left, so probably soon. You need any help with anything?"

"Can you set the table?"

I get the plates and glasses and put them around our four person table, leaving what was usually my dad's place empty. When I enter the kitchen again for silverware, Mom stops me by placing a hand on my shoulder.

"I'm really happy you have someone."

I smile. "Me too, Mom. I really like him."

She playfully smacks me as she goes back to cooking. "I can tell. You seem happier."

"How are you doing?" I ask.

"You know? I'm okay. I had a minor breakdown this morning, because I'm used to your dad complaining about me getting up early and waking him up, but also requesting I make him a lemon cake." She takes a breath. "But then I remembered how he was the only one who ate that nasty cake, and now I can make any cake I want. So I'm making strawberry cake." She gives me a small grin. "Grief comes and goes, like waves, you know? Sometimes it's not so bad and easy to tread, other times it feels like the waves are crashing over my head and trying to drown me. Either way, I wake up a little happier, and now that I secured the job with Mr. Anderson I'm feeling pretty good."

Dex came through and got his dad to hire my mom. She's a little more carefree now that she doesn't have to stress about job interviews or worry she'll never have a paycheck again. Dex's dad pays well, but it definitely comes with long hours. Mom hasn't worked there long, but she hasn't complained yet.

I kiss the top of her head right before the doorbell rings.

"Food's almost ready," she says as I make my way to the door.

When I open it up, Trevor's on the porch with his back toward me. He's wearing a pair of khaki-colored chinos that make his ass look fantastic. When he spins around with a smile on his face, I take in the light green button up shirt that highlights his eyes, and the way it fits him like it was tailor made for him only.

"Wow. You're making me feel completely underdressed." I lean to kiss him and whisper, "And beyond turned on."

He chuckles. "You look good. What're you talking about?"

I glance down at my jeans and T-shirt. "Right. Well, I'm definitely changing before we go to your parents house."

When we step inside, Mom pops around the corner. "Hey, Trevor. Wow, you look good. Food's almost ready, okay?"

"Yes, ma'am. Thank you."

It doesn't take long before we're all seated around the table, eating and talking.

"How's school?" Mom asks us both.

"Pretty good," Trevor answers. "I struggled a bit with chemistry, but other than that I'm doing okay."

Mom nods. "What are you planning on doing after school?"

I listen intently, because it's something we've actually never talked about.

"Well, it's changed a few times, but I think I've settled on being a teacher. Probably middle or high school."

"That's a good one. Not nearly appreciated enough, but I think you'd be a great influence on people's lives."

He grins. "I hope so." His eyes flicker to mine. "What about you?"

My mom smiles, reaching over to touch my arm. "Dominic's gonna be a therapist."

"Oh yeah?" he asks, digging his fork into some mashed potatoes. "What kind?"

"A child therapist."

He nods, his eyes lingering on me for a while. He knows why I'd choose that, based on what I've told him about my own childhood.

"Both of you wanting to work with kids and have an impact on their lives is amazing," Mom says. "I'm proud of you both."

Once we finish our meal, including having some strawberry cake for dessert, Mom heads over to Ms. Anne's house with an array of food, and me and Trevor get some time to hang out alone.

"I probably shouldn't have eaten as much as I did," I complain as I rub my stomach. "Gonna need to work out extra hard tomorrow."

"Besides the stuff we do for football, what do you do to work out?"

"I run when I have time, and do any and everything I can at home. Sit-ups, pushups, shit like that. I used to be better at going to the gym all the time, but I've been preoccupied," I say, giving him a wink.

"Oh, it's me that's kept you preoccupied? Not transferring schools, moving to a different town, acing all your homework, working, and playing football?"

I shake my head. "Nope. Just you. It's a lot of work to get the closeted kid who says he hates you to admit he really wants you."

He shoves me. "Shut up."

I wrap an arm around him as we sit on the couch and laugh. "I'm glad my hard work paid off."

He's quiet for a minute before he speaks up. "Why did you try?"

"What?"

"I'll admit you made some efforts in getting and keeping my attention. I kept trying to push you away, but you didn't let me. Especially after saying you didn't want to start anything with me when you first saw me in the locker room."

I grin. "I was full of shit. You said I was a drunken mistake. I wasn't about to let that go without having a response. I loved that you came in my hand so fast. Means you were really into it."

A light red color stretches across his cheeks. "Let's not bring that up again."

"Look, I'll be honest. I was really attracted to you the first night we met. I wanted to fuck you right there in that bathroom. When I saw you in the locker room, I figured the universe was finally giving me some good juju or something. I needed to try to get you alone again." I take a breath. "Focusing my attention on you was a good way to keep me from thinking about all the bad shit that was happening around me. I know that doesn't sound the greatest, but you were this little bright light in my darkness. Even all your moody bullshit." He makes a face, making me grin, but I continue. "When we're together, you give me this sense of control I need. You yield to me in a way that makes my dick hard just thinking about it. And yet, I know I'd do absolutely anything for you. In that way, you have a type of control over me. We're perfect for each other. I told you that." I rub a hand down my face, not used to spilling my guts like this. "Eventually, I realized it was more than me just wanting to fuck you. I liked being around you. I've never chased after someone before. From the get-go, I knew something was different about you." I shrug, feeling weird. "Anyway, I don't know. Does that answer your question?"

His eyes stare deeply into mine, and I can't quite read the emotion in them. Shock? Awe? He grabs my face with one hand and presses his lips to mine. We stay connected for several seconds, and he plants a few more soft kisses on me.

"Thank you," he says quietly, still holding on to my face.

We don't get to discuss this further, because Mom comes back in, but I hope we can get back to this later.

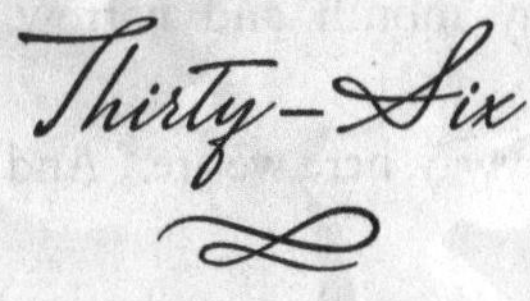

Thirty-Six

DOMINIC

"WOW," I say as we pull into his parents' driveway. "Is this where you grew up?"

He shakes his head as he parks. "No, they moved here several years ago."

I rub my palms over my pants—a pair of navy blue chinos and not jeans. I make sure the collar on my white polo is down, and scrutinize my hair in the mirror.

Trevor laughs. "Dominic Hernandez. Are you nervous?"

"Fuck off."

"I never thought I'd see you nervous."

"I've never done this. Parents?" I shake my head. "I feel like my heart is in my stomach."

Trevor reaches out and touches my thigh. "They're gonna love you. Don't worry."

I take a deep breath and blow it out. "Okay, let's go before I decide to bolt down the street."

As we head up the pathway to the door, I ask, "Are you not scared?"

"Less nervous than I thought I'd be, but the nerves are still there. They took the news really well, and I've talked to them a couple times on the phone since." He exhales. "But yeah, this is the first time I've brought someone home, so I'm kind of freaking out, but I guess one of us needs to be the brave one."

I screw up my mouth and narrow my eyes at him. "Anyway."

He laughs. "Anyway, here we are." And he opens the door and walks in.

His parents aren't anywhere to be seen right away, so we walk out of the small foyer, and pass a small sitting room to our right that looks like it was set up by one of those HGTV shows. As we keep walking, I realize the entire house looks like it's been staged for a magazine shoot. Everything is organized and tidy, but it doesn't feel stiff. It's definitely a warm, homey atmosphere.

Trevor heads for the kitchen where there's the sound of dishes clinking and water running. I once again rub my palms on the sides of my pants, taking a deep breath.

"Hey," he greets.

"Oh, Trevor, I didn't hear you come in," his mom says, putting a knife down and wiping her hands on a towel.

Her eyes bounce over his shoulder and land on me so I give her a smile.

His dad turns the water off and dries his hands before spinning around with a wide grin. "Hey, son. Happy Thanksgiving."

"Happy Thanksgiving," he replies, stepping to the side and looking back at me. "This is Dominic."

"Of course. Dominic, it's so nice to meet you," his mom offers, coming around their massive island and holding her hand out.

"It's nice to meet you, too. I love your house."

She smiles and Trevor's dad comes to shake my hand next.

"Thank you. I'm Marshall, and this is Michelle. We're happy to have you join us this year."

"Thanks for having me."

Trevor clearly got his dad's eyes, but he's a good mix of both his parents.

"Well, I was just about to take the food to the table if you want to help," his dad tells me.

"Of course."

"Trevor, will you help with this?" his mom asks, heading over to the oven.

As I pick up a couple of dishes and follow his dad through a doorway leading to a dining room, I hear his mom whisper, "He's cute," to Trevor, and I can't fight the smile on my face as relief washes over me.

Once we get all the food transferred to the table, we fill our plates and sit down.

"So, Dominic, Trevor told us a little about you. You're on the football team, too?"

"Yes, ma'am."

"But you're new to town?" his dad questions, plunging his fork into some mac and cheese.

"Well, it's my first year at South River, but I used to live not far from there when I was younger."

"And your parents? Do they still live nearby?" his dad asks.

Trevor's head comes up and he says, "Uh." He looks at me. "Sorry, I didn't mention anything about that."

I give him a small grin. "It's fine." I look at his parents. "My dad died recently, and that's what brought me back. My mom lives in South River. They moved there while I was in college at Grand Valley."

"I'm so sorry," his mom says, her hand going to her chest.

"Yes, that's awful. Sorry to hear that," his dad adds.

I give them a nod, not needing to tell them my true feelings. "Thank you. It's okay."

After only a brief lull in conversation after that mood killer, the conversation moves on and we talk about school, future plans, and then they ask a question that has me going stiff.

"How did you two meet?"

My eyes widen slightly, and luckily I had just taken a bite, so now I have a little time before being forced to answer. I glance at Trevor, hoping he'll take the lead. They probably don't want to hear the truth.

"Uh, well, Jay and I had gone to Grand Valley to go to a party at one of the frats," he says. "Dominic was there, too. We had a brief run-in there, and then he showed up in the locker room at South River Monday afternoon."

I swallow my food and see his mom smiling while his dad nods along while chewing.

"And were you friends first?" she asks.

"Honey," his dad says, giving her a look.

"What? Is that too personal?"

I laugh. "No, it's okay. We weren't really friends right away," I answer, looking at Trevor.

"I was dealing with my own issues," Trevor admits.

"Of course," his mom says with a sympathetic expression. "Well, I'm glad you two found each other and realized there was something between you. Sometimes we let outside opinions affect the decisions we make, when really it only matters how we feel."

"And I finally feel like myself. I'm happy," Trevor says.

"That's good, sweetie," his mom replies.

~

Once we've finished eating, we make our way to the living room where we gather around the TV and put on a movie. His parents sit together on the couch, leaving me and Trevor on the loveseat. I drape an arm across the back of the couch, and he scooches closer, resting a hand on my thigh. I smile and plant a quick kiss on his temple.

We don't watch the entire movie, because we all end up talking again and stop paying attention. However, I really like his parents. They make me feel like I belong and that's a great feeling. I hate that I was so nervous that they wouldn't like me, because they're some of the coolest people I've met.

It's nearing nine o'clock when Trevor yawns and stretches. "I guess we should head back. I'm feeling the effects of two Thanksgivings."

"Don't fall asleep while you're driving," his mom says.

"It's only thirty minutes."

"It only takes thirty seconds for some people to fall asleep," she says, glancing at her husband.

"I'll be fine," Trevor says with a chuckle, standing up.

"I can drive so he can get some beauty rest," I offer, getting up from the couch.

His parents laugh and Trevor elbows me.

"Please come visit again," his mom says.

"We will," Trevor replies.

"Christmas?"

The hopeful tone of her voice has me answering, because I couldn't imagine turning her down. "We'll be here."

Trevor glances at me and smiles, and his parents get up to say goodbye.

"Be safe," his mom says as she hugs Trevor. "I love you."

"I love you, too."

She steps to me next, wrapping her arms around me. "Thank you for making my son happy."

"I'd do anything for him," I reply as I hug her back.

She gives me a squeeze before his dad comes to shake my hand and pat me on the shoulder.

On the way to the car, Trevor grabs my hand and tugs me closer to give me a kiss. "I told you they'd love you."

"Guess I'm pretty loveable," I answer with a shrug. "Now give me the keys, sleeping beauty. I'll get us back home."

He tosses them to me without a fight and climbs into the passenger seat. I start up the car and give him another look. "We survived a holiday with the parents. Isn't that a pretty big milestone?"

With a snort, he says, "I think so. Let's see if we make it through Christmas."

As soon as I pull onto the street, he leans his head against the window and closes his eyes. I keep peeking over at him, a smile stuck on my face. I squeeze his thigh before I put both hands on the wheel and focus on the road.

He shifts slightly and murmurs, "I love you."

I do a double take, then a triple. Did I hear him correctly? Is he already dreaming? He doesn't open his eyes or move again.

I spend the rest of the drive home trying to decipher what else it could've been. Did he mean it? Do I ask him about it? No, definitely not. He probably doesn't even know he said it, and how would that conversation go? *Hey, I think you said you loved me before you drifted off to sleep? Do you?*

And how would I respond if he said yes? Because if I'm being honest, I've had a few moments where I've definitely wondered if how I'm feeling is love. I wouldn't really know. There's not a set list of things you must feel in order to decipher if you're in love or not.

I know I love being around him. I love making him laugh. I love seeing him smile. I love that he's been so brave with telling his family and friends about his sexuality, and about me. I love that he was so intent on not letting another man touch me, that he publicly came out to people in order to say I was his. I love how he looks at me. I love the way he blushes when I tell him all the dirty things I want to do to him. I love how he makes me feel. I love how happy I've felt since I've known him.

I think I love him.

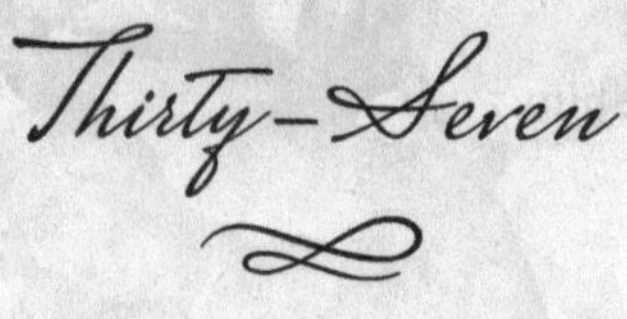

Thirty-Seven

DOMINIC

A LITTLE OVER three weeks go by without either of us mentioning that four letter word—love. He never acts uncomfortable or nervous, so I don't think he's aware he said it. But it's all I can think about.

We spend nearly every day together. If I'm not working, I'm with him. Most of our days are full. We have school, practice, football games, and then I go to my job from early evening to early in the morning. We've been to a few more parties as a couple, but I've just realized I've never taken him out on a proper date.

"Hey, Trev," I yell from the bathroom.

"Yeah?" He pops in a few seconds later, looking sexy as fuck in only a pair of basketball shorts, his hair still wet from the shower.

"I'm off on Saturday. I'm taking you on a date."

His bright eyes and wide smile make my heart stutter in my chest. "Yeah?"

"I don't know why we haven't done it yet."

He shrugs. "We stay pretty busy."

"Well, clear your schedule."

"Done."

"Come kiss me."

He saunters in and kisses me. "Done."

"Mm. I like this game. Touch me."

His eyes drop to the towel around my waist, and with one quick movement the towel falls and his hand wraps around my cock. "Done." His voice is breathier now.

"Kiss me again." When he leans in to push his lips to mine, I pull back. "Lower."

His teeth drag across his bottom lip before he drops to his knees and plants teasing kisses across my lower stomach. "Here?" he asks, mischief in his eyes.

"You know where."

His soft lips leave small kisses on my shaft, his eyes flickering up to me right before his tongue snakes out and licks the underside of my erection.

"Oh fuck," I groan. He takes me to the back of his throat and I hunch over, placing my hand on the counter behind him. "I love being in your mouth."

He moans before reaching a hand into his shorts to stroke himself.

"Get up," I say, helping him. "Drop the shorts and turn around."

While he does that, I rush into his bedroom and grab the lube and bring it back to the bathroom. I'm dying to be inside him, so I make quick work of prepping him before I slather the liquid on my cock.

"Watch me fuck you," I tell him, making eye contact in the mirror.

I slide in, holding onto his hips while I move in and out. His face contorts, his teeth sinking into his bottom lip while his head drops back, exposing his neck. I watch his Adam's apple bob as he swallows, and then his lips part as he gasps.

"Fuck, you're beautiful."

His head comes down and our gazes connect. I lean over his back and kiss his neck before nibbling my way to his collarbone, all while my hips rock back and forth, taking me in and out of his tight hole.

"God, you feel so good," I breathe.

He moans, and I stand up straight and lift his knee to rest on the counter.

"Oh God, Dominic," he pants, his head dropping down and his muscles flexing in his back as he grips the side of the counter. "Fuck, baby," he whispers.

"Tell me how it feels," I growl.

"So good," he says between moans. "You fuck me so good."

I growl and grip him tighter, moving a little faster. "I love being inside you. I love...everything about you."

He makes a noise between a gasp and a cry, and I go harder and deeper, but keep the pace steady. He reaches between his legs and starts stroking his dick.

"Oh fuck," I roar, my orgasm hitting hard. I'm nothing but moans and gasps after that, my body nearly going limp afterwards.

Trevor makes the sexiest noises as he strokes himself, watching me come apart behind him. I pull out and spin him around, dropping to my knees in front of him. "In my mouth," I say. "Come in my mouth."

With one hand on my head, he strokes himself until his eyes close and his mouth opens wide as he cries out. "Shit."

Warm liquid hits my tongue and then I take his crown in my mouth and lick and suck until he's given me every last drop.

When I stand up, there's something in the way he looks at me that gives me pause. He's studying me carefully, and whatever he's thinking seems to be on the tip of his tongue, but he doesn't say anything. I have a feeling it's what I said. I said I love everything about him. It was very close to being *I love you.* He must know that loving everything about someone has to mean something.

"Sorry I dirtied you up after your shower."

His lips pull up on one side. "No, you're not."

"True."

And like that, we move past it. But I have a plan.

~

When I show up to his house on Saturday night, I'm dressed in a pair of black slacks and a white button up with a black and white striped tie. Since it's winter, I'm also wearing a black overcoat.

He opens the door, looking handsome in his own pair of black pants, a gray sweater over a white collared shirt, and a black leather jacket.

I give him a slow once over. "Damn, Campbell. Lookin' good. Got plans?"

He smirks. "You can change them," he replies, reaching out and tugging me into him, kissing me like he hasn't seen me in weeks.

"Don't tempt me," I say against his lips. "Trying to do this boyfriend thing right."

I take his hand and escort him to the passenger side of my car, opening the door for him. He gives me a look like, *really?*

"Humor me."

He rolls his eyes, but his smile lets me know he's anything but annoyed. He gets in and I walk around to my side. It takes almost half an hour to get to the restaurant, but that's mostly because the roads are covered in a fresh layer of snow. It stopped a little while ago, but the trucks haven't had time to clear all the roads yet, and people are being cautious.

Downtown, where the restaurant is, buildings and businesses are lit up for Christmas. Lights twinkle in windows and on trees, and the snow really makes it look like a winter wonderland.

Once we get to the restaurant, we're taken to our table immediately. It's full of people, but we get seated in a corner that gives us a sense of privacy.

"Have you been here before?" I ask.

He shakes his head. "Nope. It's really nice though."

"Let's hope the food is nice."

The waiter arrives and takes our drink and appetizer order while we continue to look over the menu. Once we've decided on what we want and tell the waiter, I reach across the table and grab his hand.

"You look good enough to eat."

His cheeks redden. "We could've stayed home."

"But I want everyone to know you're mine," I say with a grin.

"Then I guess it's okay."

The waiter drops off our appetizer and drinks, and me and Trev talk about everything from football—both he and I are now starting every game and doing pretty damn good, to what everyone else is doing for Christmas break. Dex, Vi, Renzo, and Ronan are apparently taking a trip together, and Jay is going to visit his family.

"My mom's thinking about moving," I tell him.

"Why? I thought she just paid a good chunk on the mortgage."

"She did, but now she's thinking she wants to live closer to town so she's closer to work. She complains about the commute, plus I think she's hit this point where she no longer cares about salvaging memories. She needs a fresh start away from a place that was so toxic.

"Makes sense."

"It'll probably take a little bit. She'll need to sell the house and hopefully get some money out of it, but with her new job, she's making enough to be able to get a small place."

He nods and then the waiter drops our food off. After we eat and talk about how good everything is, we decide to pass on dessert.

"Back home?" he asks, biting his lip briefly.

"Not yet," I say with a laugh, holding his hand as we walk back outside.

Instead of heading back to the car, I go in the opposite direction, and we stroll hand-in-hand on the sidewalk, looking at all the window displays and eventually come to the winter garden area.

The trees are completely covered in different lights, and pathways are marked with ground lights, guiding you as you enjoy all the Christmas pop-ups. There's snowmen, reindeer, and little cottages where you can stop for hot cocoa or cider. Kids gather around one house where Santa and Mrs. Clause are, taking pictures.

"I love this," he says, squeezing my hand. "Guess I'm still a kid at heart."

"Who doesn't enjoy Christmas lights?"

We get to a part where there's a few benches surrounding an outdoor heater, so I sit him down next to me and shift to face him.

"Thank you for this," he says before I can say anything. "Thank you for everything." He looks at me then, his eyes studying my face.

"You don't have to thank me. I want you to be happy."

"Well, I am. With you, I always am."

I hold his chin between my thumb and forefinger and give him a kiss. "I think you make me a better person."

When a few snowflakes begin to fall, I decide this is a better time than any. I open my mouth to say the three words I've been dying to say for a little while now.

"I love you."

I blink at him, my lips parted, because he said it at the same time I did.

We both chuckle a little. "What did you say?" I ask.

"I love you."

"No, I love *you*."

He laughs. "We love each other."

I grab his face and kiss him. When I pull away, I hold his hand and put it on my thigh.

"God, I've been holding it in. I couldn't take it anymore."

"I thought it was just me," he says, exhaling loudly. We study each other, our matching wide smiles plastered on our faces. "You love me."

"I do, and I love that you love me, too."

"Can I show you how much?" he asks, spreading his fingers across my thigh.

"Oh, baby. You can spend all night showing me how much, and I'll spend as long as you'll let me, proving that I do."

"Oh God. Let's go home. Santa and these kids don't need to see all the things I want to do to you right now."

Epilogue

TREVOR

CHRISTMAS COMES AND GOES, and we enjoy a small dinner and some presents at Dominic's house with his mom before heading to my parents' house on Christmas Day, where we exchange a few more gifts and eat even more food.

When New Year's Eve comes around, we head to Renzo's parents house, where they hold their usual party for some of their friends and their kids' friends. Like last year, the kids end up downstairs in their basement for the majority of the night, playing pool, drinking, and snacking on the food Mrs. H had prepared. Unlike last year, I'm not struggling with my sexual identity and hiding it from my friends. I'm actually attached to Dominic a majority of the night, and able to kiss him when midnight hits. It's a phenomenal feeling.

Shortly after we celebrate the new year with our closest friends, we head back to my place to enjoy more of each other alone.

Valentine's day hits, and even though I've always thought it was more of a holiday for women, we find the perfect way to celebrate. There's no flowers, teddy bears, or heart-shaped chocolate boxes, but we do go out to a restaurant for dinner, stop at a store on the way home and split up to get items we want to put to use tonight.

At home, he rushes to the bedroom with his bags, and I stay in the living room, putting my gifts together. He comes out nearly fifteen minutes later with a grin on his face and a red gift bag.

"You ready to exchange?" I ask, picking up my own bag.

I hand him his gifts when he gives me mine, and we both start digging inside.

The first thing I pull from his bag is a bottle of wine. I arch a brow at him. "Wine?"

"Okay, I'm not a wine connoisseur, but a woman in the store assured me this was a good one."

I chuckle as I place it on the coffee table. "Okay, we'll crack this open soon."

He takes his first gift out of the bag, which is a small container of the caramel flavored popcorn he loves so much.

We go back and forth, removing one gift at a time. I pull out a bottle of massage oil. "You gonna massage me?"

"It will most definitely lead to sex," he says with a smirk. "Grab the next one."

The next box is a bottle of lube. I laugh. "I think we have some of this."

"Yeah, but this is pink and smells like roses, so it's Valentine themed."

I snort. "Okay, you go."

He pulls out the movie Magic Mike and cracks up. "I heard this movie wasn't that good."

"Nobody's watching for the acting."

"So, this is like foreplay. Gotcha. Don't try to get me to dance for you tonight. I'm no Channing."

"You're so much better."

When I pull out my next gift, I start laughing. It's a pair of red boxer briefs with white hearts all over them.

"You'll be wearing those when I massage you," he says, waggling his brows.

"You might also have a clothing item," I say, nodding at the bag. He removes his own pair of boxer-briefs—his white with red X's and O's. "And you'll be wearing those," I tell him.

He grins. "Great minds."

When all is said and done, we end up with conversation hearts and red-only Jolly Ranchers to add to everything else.

"So, we're gonna change into our new boxer-briefs, put on Magic Mike, snack on some popcorn and drink wine, then I'll massage you while you eat those nasty conversation hearts and I suck on some Jolly Ranchers, then we go to the bedroom where we'll put the lube to use. It's a perfect night," he says with a grin.

"Sounds like a plan, except..."

"Except what?"

"I have one more surprise gift. One that didn't come from the store."

"But those were the rules," he says, giving me a look. "Only things from the store."

I shrug, looking sheepish as I bite my lip. "I'm sorry, but I hope you still like it."

After rushing to the kitchen and grabbing the small white box from one of the drawers, I head back to a very confused looking Dominic who hesitantly takes the box from me.

Before he opens it, his eyes flicker to mine. My stomach is in knots as my heart pounds in my chest. I hope this isn't a stupid idea that ruins what was a perfect Valentine's Day.

When he sees what's inside, he stares at it for a few seconds before meeting my gaze again. "You...what is this? I mean, I think I know, but..."

I step up to him and take one of his hands in mine. "It

makes sense. You're always here, and I love having you around."

"You want me to move in?"

With a smile, I say, "Yes, I want you to move in."

"Are you sure?" he asks, glancing at the key then back at me.

"Definitely, but don't feel like you have to if you don't want to."

He tosses the box to the table and takes me in his arms. "No, of course I want to."

"Yeah?" I ask, my grin growing stupidly wide.

"My mom will be moving anyway, and I'd rather be here with you than at some apartment by myself. Plus, I kinda love you."

I playfully pinch him before stepping back. "Kinda?"

"You're everything to me, Trev. You know that," he replies, wrapping his arms around my waist and kissing my forehead.

I feel my cheeks heat up as I grin. "I guess that's better."

He smacks my ass before beginning to tug me toward the hall. "I'm really glad you walked in on me in the bathroom all those months ago."

With a laugh, I say, "I'm really glad it was you that was in there. Who knows how my story would've gone if it wasn't for you."

Dominic pulls me through the doorway to my room. Our room. "I think we're gonna have to postpone the movie for a little bit."

"What do you have in mind?"

"A lifetime of things," he answers, a small grin on his lips. "But for now, let me taste you." Then he drops to his knees and starts undoing my pants.

"God, I love you," I whisper, running a hand through his hair.

Acknowledgments

Thank you for reading! I hope you enjoyed Trev and Dom's journey. I loved them from the beginning and had so much fun writing their story. Please take a minute to leave a review if you can.

I want to thank my husband, because he reads every single book I put out, and helps me polish them up. I wouldn't want to do this, or life, without you. Thanks for always being a listening ear when I need to vent, rant, ramble, or discuss what I want to do with these fictional characters. You're truly the best. I appreciate you so much. I love you.

To Robin from Wicked by Design for creating my covers and making graphics for stickers and swag, and always bringing what I have in mind to life. You're simply amazing.

Huge thanks to Cass Thomasson for all the work you put into my ARC team and helping me with my books. I adore you!

Aundi, you are a new member to the beta team and I'm thrilled to have you and your notes. You were beyond helpful, and those edits you make?? I bow down to you.

To the rest of the beta team, thank you for taking time out to read my story when it's in its roughest stage.

Candi from Candi Kane PR—you are amazing at your job. I'm so appreciative of your work and dedication.

To every reader and blogger who reads, reviews, and shares my book, I'll never be able to thank you enough. I couldn't do this without you. Thank you, thank you, thank you!

To my author friends who've helped me by sharing, or

doing swaps with me, I appreciate your kindness. We're in this together, and I love that I have people I can count on.

I still feel like I'm missing someone, or multiple people, but know that I'm grateful for each and every person who worked on my book, read my book, shared and reviewed my book, or even just gave me a chance.

Isabel Lucero is a bestselling author, finding joy in giving readers books for every mood.

Born in a small town in New Mexico, Isabel was lucky enough to escape and travel the world thanks to her husband's career in the Air Force. She and her husband have three kids and two dogs together, and currently reside in Delaware. When Isabel isn't on mommy duty or writing her next book, she can be found reading, or in the nearest Target buying things she doesn't need. Isabel loves connecting with her readers and fans of books in general. Keep in touch!

Sign up for my newsletter.
Join my reading group.

Also by Isabel Lucero

Think Again
Darkness Within
Splintered
Dysfunctional
Twisted Valentine
The Prince of Darkness
Lights, Camera, Passion

The Kingston Brothers Series
On the Rocks
Truth or Dare
Against the Rules
Risking it All

South River University Series
Stealing Ronan
Tasting Innocence
Breaking Free
Tempting Him